NOAH'S CHOICE

Since the death of the last Dodo three centuries ago, the human race has been responsible for bringing about the extinction of hundreds of animal species. In the last century, however, there are many who have chosen to save rather than destroy them. Like latter-day children of the biblical Noah, these people have given safe refuge to many of the thousands of animal species now threatened by the rising flood-tide of extinction.

Noah's Choice tells of the tragic but fascinating events which resulted in such infamous extinctions as the Dodo, and of the terrible slaughter of animals as diverse as the huge Steller's Sea Cow and the tiny Hawaiian Honeycreeper bird. But we also hear heartening stories of animals such as the American Bison and the Grey Whale, which were rescued from the very brink of extinction.

David Day is a Canadian poet and author whose books have sold over half a million copies in one hundred countries and have been translated into a dozen languages. He has published several books of poems, publications on natural history and children's books. His landmark book on animal extinction, *The Doomsday Book of Animals* (recently reissued as *The Encyclopedia of Vanished Species*), was the critics' Book of the Year choice for both *Time* magazine and the *Observer*. David Day also writes a weekly column for *Punch*.

Noah's Choice

True Stories of
Extinction and Survival

DAVID DAY

Illustrated by Mick Loates

PUFFIN BOOKS

To Brian and Mariette

PUFFIN BOOKS

Published by the Penguin Group
Penguin Books Ltd, 27 Wrights Lane, London W8 5TZ, England
Penguin Books USA Inc., 375 Hudson Street, New York, New York 10014, USA
Penguin Books Australia Ltd, Ringwood, Victoria, Australia
Penguin Books Canada Ltd, 10 Alcorn Avenue, Toronto, Ontario, Canada M4V 3B2
Penguin Books (NZ) Ltd, 182–190 Wairau Road, Auckland 10, New Zealand

Penguin Books Ltd, Registered Offices: Harmondsworth, Middlesex, England

First published by Viking 1990
Published in Puffin Books 1991
1 3 5 7 9 10 8 6 4 2

Researcher: Jane Smith
Text copyright © David Day, 1990
Illustrations copyright © Mick Loates, 1990
All rights reserved

The moral right of the author has been asserted

Printed in England by Clays Ltd, St Ives plc
Set in Linotron Imprint

Except in the United States of America, this book is sold subject
to the condition that it shall not, by way of trade or otherwise, be lent,
re-sold, hired out, or otherwise circulated without the publisher's
prior consent in any form of binding or cover other than that in
which it is published and without a similar condition including this
condition being imposed on the subsequent purchaser

AUGUSTANA LIBRARY
UNIVERSITY OF ALBERTA

If all the beasts were gone,
Men would die from great loneliness of spirit.
Whatever happens to the beast, happens to man.

All things are connected.
Whatever befalls the earth,
Befalls the sons of the earth.

– Chief Seattle

Contents

LIST OF ILLUSTRATIONS

INTRODUCTION

For a moment, let us imagine it is the Age of the Dinosaurs once again. The Tyrannosaurus Rex stampedes through the jungle after its hopeless, fleeing prey. The Pterodactyl soars across the primeval sky. The towering Brontosaurus wades through the steaming tropical swamp.

Now imagine that you are an Alien from another planet who has just landed in this prehistoric world. Your leaders have learned that a huge meteor will soon collide with the Earth. It is likely to destroy all forms of animal life on the planet's surface. You have been sent on a mission of mercy.

You are a kind of intergalactic Noah with a huge Space Ark. You have been told you must choose the most important animals on the planet, load them into the Space Ark, then leave the planet. Immediately after the disaster, you may return to the planet, and release the animals. In this way it is hoped you will be ensuring the continued survival of life on the planet.

The great and crucial question is: of all the giant and numerous creatures on this teeming tropical planet, which animals would you choose?

It is a difficult question. If you were a logical sort of Alien, you would undoubtedly choose a great number of the larger, more obvious life forms. In the balance of things, you would probably NOT choose (if indeed you even noticed it) a tiny mouse-like rodent scurrying through the rotting vegetation. Indeed, in the Age of the

Dinosaurs, there is no doubt it was a totally insignificant creature.

But if you had missed it, what would the consequences have been? In order to make an even more extreme case, let us go so far as to say that you saved every animal on the planet, but simply overlooked this three-inch long rodent.

Let us see. By virtue of the advanced technology of your sophisticated Alien civilization, you are given the ability to time-travel into the planet's future so you can survey the results of your mission of mercy. You set your instruments, and in a flash you arrive in our present age at the end of the twentieth century.

How would you feel about this strange new world? No doubt you would be pleased at your decision to save the flying reptiles which have evolved into the thousands of species of birds in the world. You would also be delighted by the variety and number of fishes that fill the seas and lakes. However, there is no doubt you would be saddened by the disappearance of the amazing giant reptiles, which have been reduced to a mere handful of tiny crocodiles, lizards and tortoises.

You might whimsically reflect on the vast emptiness of this world's land masses but, as an Alien, you wouldn't miss or expect to see what would be most obvious to a Human observer: there would be no people on the planet. In fact, there would be no mammals of any kind at all on the globe.

As an Alien, of course, you could not have known that one seemingly insignificant rodent was to become the ancestor of all mammals, including that animal called *Homo sapiens*, a species that would eventually have evolved into a being capable of creating a technology nearly as advanced as your own.

*

Having imagined all this, you might now wish to return to your human form. The point of this little fantasy is simply to propose a rather different and more far-reaching way of viewing the consequences of extinction.

At this point in history, it is clear we are in exactly the same position as our Alien Noah. Thousands of animals are endangered and threatened with extinction. There is no doubt that their fate is in our hands. Whether we wish to or not, we are daily making choices which will determine the fate of hundreds of species.

It is a heavy responsibility, and it is important to see that, like our Alien Noah in the Dinosaur Age, our actions will have consequences in the future we cannot even imagine.

We cannot know what plans evolution has for us and life on this planet. (Who could have predicted the mouse would overthrow the dinosaur?) We may well ask what creature – small, timid, unseen – will rise up, long after we are gone, and inherit the planet.

There is no way of telling, but surely there is something deeply wise in the human heart when a murmuring sentiment tells us that the needless extermination of entire species is an absolute evil that must be avoided at all costs.

This book is divided into two parts: EXTINCTION and SURVIVAL.

The first half is a collection of cautionary tales. It deals with animal species that have already become extinct. These are tragic cases, and you may find the reasons animals have become extinct are sad, strange and baffling. However, it is important to know them. For, as it is often said, those who do not learn from tragedies of history are destined to repeat them.

The second part deals with animals that seemed destined to become extinct, but have miraculously survived.

Again, it may be said that the facts are often strange and the lessons valuable. This part of the book proves that individuals' actions do make a difference, and it celebrates the victories some of these individuals have achieved.

PART ONE

Extinction

CHAPTER I

The Fable of the Dodo

Dodos and Solitaires

'Once upon a time, on an island far away, there was the strangest bird you've ever seen. It was large and round, and had a rather weirdly comic face. It had wings, but was so fat it could not fly. It was so stupid, it did not have the sense to flee its enemies. It is no surprise that soon after its discovery, this ridiculous bird became extinct.'

This is a brief potted version of what passes for a typical history of that creature we call the Dodo (*Raphus cucullatus*). However, this is a view of the bird that is neither fair to the animal nor historically accurate.

In the three centuries since its extinction, the Dodo has become as much of a mythical animal as a unicorn or a dragon. Because of its seemingly awkward and comic shape, and the manner in which it so rapidly became extinct after its discovery, it has become the butt of many a joke: 'Dead as a Dodo' and 'Dumb as a Dodo' are as commonplace as 'Sly as a Fox' and 'Meek as a Lamb'.

It is a pointless exercise to defend this long-lost animal from such jibes, but there is some importance in learning from the errors of history. Unfortunately, as it is usually told, the history of the Dodo is not so much history as an extremely misleading fable about obsolete evolutionary design. The Dodo is generally shown as the classic example of that much misinterpreted phrase 'survival of the fittest'. This fable of the Dodo implies that the animal was simply 'unfit' for survival and, far from being tragic, there was a moral 'rightness' in its extinction.

It is a view of history that allows us to forget the circumstances behind the Dodo's case and the human role in its extinction. It argues that it was a law of nature itself that exterminated the Dodo. It is a view that ignores the fact that the Dodo had survived on this planet for sixty million years before it encountered the human race. This is some thirty times longer than humans have been on earth. How could such an 'unfit' animal survive so long?

This convenient interpretation of the idea of 'survival of the fittest' as presented in this modern 'fable of the Dodo' has been used to justify the hundreds of other man-caused animal extinctions that have occurred over the last three centuries. It is a view that is impossible to uphold with any honesty if we look at the actual historic facts. In almost every case, but for the actions of the human race, there is no doubt that all these species would still survive today.

Still, a very good place to begin to review the natural history of extinction over the last three centuries is with that most infamous of cases: the Dodo.

Six hundred miles off the east coast of Madagascar lies an isolated trio of beautiful islands known as the Mascarenes – Mauritius, Réunion and Rodriguez. Set alone in the Indian Ocean, the islands were rarely visited by man until early in the sixteenth century. In common with many other remote islands, no mammals lived on the Mascarenes, leaving the birds there free to live without fear of predators. In time, the birds came to dominate the islands, taking advantage of their remarkably safe, isolated

Dodo   *Raphus cucullatus*

habitat to evolve into many strange, wonderful species. One of these species was the Dodo.

Strange as it may seem, the Dodo was actually a giant form of flightless dove. At 23kg (50lb) in weight it was about the size of two turkeys, and certainly the largest 'pigeon' to inhabit the earth. The Dodo had a large head which was only partially feathered. It had a strong, hooked beak and its large body was rounded and feathered with a soft, dark down. It had strong, stout legs and small, flightless wings. The Dodo was extremely dove-like and gentle in its temperament and yet for tens of millions of years it not only survived, but became one of the dominant life forms in this island paradise of Mauritius.

When the Portuguese arrived on Mauritius in 1507, the Dodos had never seen man, or any form of predatory mammal, before. Living as they did, on a lonely island inhabited mostly by birds, they had no fear whatever. When the sailors came ashore from these first tall ships, the Dodos came wandering out of the undergrowth and on to the beach to inspect these curious-looking creatures. The reaction of the sailors was immediate: they slaughtered the trusting, inquisitive birds on sight.

The Dodos' innocent, curious nature was neither unique nor due to stupidity: in sixty million years they had never experienced anything more aggressive than the plant-eating giant tortoises that crawled up on the island's beaches. Similar reactions of numerous species were frequently recorded by travellers to uninhabited tropical islands. Furthermore, it is a curious fact that, in every case, when European travellers came upon a tropical island that had never been visited by humans before, they constantly delighted in exclaiming that they had found an idyllic paradise. They would then immediately set about slaughtering its every inhabitant.

Typical was this remarkable account written in 1788 by

Surgeon Arthur Bowes aboard the British ship *Lady Penrhyn* that visited a newly discovered tropical island: 'When I was in the woods among the birds I could not help picturing myself in the Golden Age described by Ovid – all these birds walking totally fearless and unconcerned in all parts around us so that we had nothing more to do than stand still a minute or two and knock down as many as we pleased, if you missed they would never run away. The pigeons were so tame they would sit upon the branches of the trees till you might go and take them off with your hands. Many hundreds of parrots and paroquets, magpies and other birds were caught and carried aboard our ship.'

Another sailor, Captain Thomas Charlotte, in another British ship called the *Charlotte* but on the same expedition as Surgeon Bowes, also wrote about the birds on that island on the same day: 'Several of these I knocked down, and their legs being broken, I placed them near me as I sat under a tree. The pain they suffered caused them to make a doleful cry which brought five or six dozen of the same kind to them and by that means I was able to take nearly the whole of them.'

Nearly a century after the Portuguese, the Dutch came to Mauritius in 1598 to continue the destruction of the species. Again, the birds were used as a ready supply of fresh food for the sailors, with reports of forty or fifty of these large birds being taken aboard the ships in a single day.

However, it was not just the sailors who destroyed the Dodos. As the ships arrived they brought with them rats, dogs, cats, pigs and even monkeys. Over the years, more and more of these invading animals were left behind and bred on the island. At one point, the rat population of Mauritius was so great that the entire human population was forced to flee the island. Another time, the imported

pigs were causing so much damage to the forests and farms
that the human inhabitants of the island organized a hunt
in which 1,500 wild pigs were killed in a single day.

The threat to the Dodos was increasing: their nests,
built on the ground, left their eggs within easy reach of all
the newly introduced predators. The defenceless chicks
were easy prey for the cats and rats. Even the large adult
birds were killed as the dogs hunted them out – unable to
fly, they could not escape. By 1680, the Mauritian Dodo
was extinct.

That, however, is not quite the end of the story of the
Dodo. Few people realize there were once three other
distinct Dodo species. One was an animal that was rather
like an albino form which was simply called the White
Dodo (*Victorionis imperialis*), and the other two were
more distant cousins, called the Réunion Solitaire
(*Ornithaptera solitarius*) and the Rodriguez Solitaire
(*Pezohaps solitarius*).

The White Dodo lived in the more remote and
mountainous regions of neighbouring Réunion, and consequently outlived the Mauritian Dodo by ninety years. It
did not become extinct until 1770. The two Dodo relatives
called Solitaires were of a similar size to the Dodos, but
were never considered stupid, ugly or awkward animals.
In fact, they were described as being rather elegant, swan-
like birds capable of considerable speed who, if need be,
could become aggressive in defence of themselves or their
young. These features notwithstanding, the Réunion
Solitaire became extinct in 1700, while the Rodriguez
Solitaire lasted out until 1800. Interestingly enough, it
appears that several Dodos of various species were sent as
live specimens to a number of European collectors. It is a
great tragedy that these birds were not thought sufficiently
important to be bred in captivity. Instead, they were

displayed as mere curiosities. Had the collectors who received them tried to do so, they might still be with us. However doomed they were in their natural habitat, it would surely have been possible to keep them safely in zoos or parks. That the Dodos managed to survive the long, arduous sea journey that brought them to Europe indicated that they were tough, hardy creatures. From all accounts they adapted well to their new circumstances and there is nothing to indicate that they were not capable of breeding in captivity.

There is one poignant record of a Dodo being exhibited in London in 1638. Sir Hamon Lestrange saw a poster advertising this strange bird and went to see it for himself. He wrote later that he saw a huge bird, bigger than a turkey, which the keeper referred to as a Dodo. The keeper was at pains to point out the food of the Dodo, which was simply a pile of large stones in the corner of the bird's enclosure. Dodos certainly did eat a few pebbles, holding them in their gizzards to crush their food with; but the picture of that one lonely Dodo, confined to a small cage in a dark London house thousands of miles away from the sunny Mascarenes, being fed from a heap of stones and surrounded all day by hordes of curious people, is a sad one.

So, what lesson can we learn from the Dodo's extinction?

It is undoubtedly true that certain biological character-istics and geographical circumstances make some species more susceptible to extinction than others. But the sudden invasion and exploitation of the Mascarene Islands was so ruthless and extreme, it is ridiculous to blame the Dodo for its inability to adapt. Adaptability, speed, intelligence, and the ability to fight, fly or flee from enemies, were found in many of the animals who now share the fate of the Dodo. As we shall see in future chapters, some of the world's most numerous and superbly 'fit' species have been obliterated just as quickly as the Dodo.

On the Mascarene Islands, in particular, the Dodo's story was far from unique. No less than twenty-eight species – Dodos, tortoises, owls, starlings, parrots, rails, lizards and snakes – have become extinct in this island paradise. Today, over 80 per cent of the islands' native wildlife species are either critically endangered or extinct.

So, it must be said, beyond everything else, there is one lesson we must learn from the Dodo's extinction, and that lesson is exactly the opposite of the one implied in' that little 'fable of the Dodo' with which we began this chapter.

The single most important acknowledgement we must make is: since the Dodo, the survival or extinction of species has NOT been determined by the laws of nature. It has been determined by the laws, economics, politics and fashions or simple whims of the human race.

CHAPTER 2

Infinite Flocks

Passenger Pigeon,
Carolina Parakeet, Great Auk

When the early explorers of the New World of the Americas returned to Europe, they were filled with stories wilder and more exciting than the strangest myths of ancient times. They claimed there were cities of gold, waterfalls that reached the skies, forests with trees thicker and taller than the greatest cathedral spires.

But the stories that most excited the European imagination were those of the limitless wildlife of the New World: fishermen being able to cross wide rivers on the backs of fish, individual bison herds covering an area the size of Scotland, flocks of birds that darkened the skies.

Of all the natural wonders of the New World, the seemingly infinite flocks of the Passenger Pigeons (*Ectopistes migratorius*) were perhaps the single most amazing phenomenon. It seems as difficult for us today as it was for Europeans of two or three centuries ago to believe the descriptions, but there is no doubt about their authenticity.

That most respected of America's early naturalists and wildlife artists, James Audubon, in autumn 1813, was travelling in a wagon from his home on the Ohio River to Louisville, Kentucky, some sixty-five kilometres away, when a column of Passenger Pigeons flew overhead.

Audubon said they literally filled the sky so that the 'light of the noonday sun was obscured as by an eclipse'. Audubon reached Louisville at sunset and the birds were still passing overhead in a solid mass. Other flocks followed the first for a further three days. The naturalist attempted to calculate the number of birds to pass overhead in just one of these flocks. He estimated that a flock of birds one and a half kilometres wide, passing overhead at a rate of one and a half kilometres per minute, for three hours, would contain 1,015,036,000 creatures. He also estimated that such a flock would consume 8,712,000 bushels of seed per day.

Another well-known naturalist, Alexander Wilson, had visited a Passenger Pigeon nesting site just a few years before Audubon, in that same area of Kentucky. The huge and densely packed forest nesting site was nearly fifty kilometres long and five or six kilometres wide. Wilson wrote of a single flight of these birds going to a nesting site of equal size, some seventy kilometres away. The Pigeons travelled at an estimated speed of one and a half kilometres a minute, high beyond reach of gunshot, very close together and many layers deep. He calculated that this flight contained 2,230,272,000 Passenger Pigeons and that such a flock would consume some 17,424,000 bushels of nuts and seeds a day.

There are scores of similar descriptions of these vast flocks. It was a species that seemed so numerous it was impossible to believe that any amount of hunting would have made any impression on the population. Passenger Pigeons seemed just a fact of life to the early Americans. Like the spring rains, the winter snows, the vast migrating flocks came and went each year.

The fact is that of all the planet's known birds, the Passenger Pigeon was the most successful and most numerous species ever to live. It is estimated that the

Passenger Pigeon once made up 40 per cent of the bird population of all of North America.

The habitat of the Passenger Pigeon seems to have included virtually the whole of forested North America, although its primary territory probably covered the land east of the Mississippi from the Hudson Bay to the Gulf of Mexico. The pigeons fed primarily on the acorns and nuts of the hardwood forests and on the seeds of coniferous woodlands. They also ate various types of grain, grass seeds, berries and small insects.

The Passenger Pigeon was a strong and beautiful bird about 30cm (1ft) long. It was also long-lived: many birds were known to live twenty-five years or more. Its head was a soft bluish grey which deepened to a metallic purple over the neck and shoulders of the bird. Its lower back and wings were grey or brown; its breast was coloured a gentle cinnamon brown which faded to white lower down. Its two centre tail feathers were dark grey and the remainder were white; it had fiery orange eyes and red feet and legs.

The great migrations of Passenger Pigeons seem to have been related to the availability of food as well as to their breeding habits. When they found plentiful supplies of food in the woodlands, they would come together; when food was more scarce, they dispersed into smaller flocks. Because of their strong, swift flying (they could maintain constant speeds of more than 96km (60 miles) per hour and fly 1,600km (1,000 miles) in a single day), they could easily find sufficient food to sustain the huge flocks.

When James Audubon visited a roosting and nesting site, he described the forest area vividly. The trees were so cluttered with the nests of the birds that dozens of branches had been broken off the trees by the extra weight: many trees, themselves more than 60cm (2ft) in diameter, were broken off a few metres from the ground, again by the weight of the nesting birds. The noise and the odour of the nesting birds was overwhelming; not a single green shoot was visible in the whole area as the birds had either eaten everything or smothered it with a covering of dung and feathers and eggshells. When the flock returned to the site, there was unbelievable confusion and uproar: the wings of so many birds were like a gale and the sound of their landing was like thunder.

The Indians of North America had hunted the Passenger Pigeon for centuries, eating the meat of the bird and using its fat as butter. They put a high value on the Pigeon and were cautious with their hunting, taking only the small number of birds that they required, being careful not to hunt while the young birds were being raised, to ensure a constant replenishment of the flocks. However, the white men who also hunted the Pigeon used no discretion when taking the birds. It seems inconceivable that a bird as numerous as the Passenger Pigeon could have been so rapidly exterminated: the determination of the men who destroyed them was as extraordinary as the numbers of their quarry.

The demand for these birds was phenomenal. In the 1850s, a single small-time New York merchant reported that he was selling 18,000 pigeons a day. There were many hundreds like him in New York, Chicago, St Louis, New Orleans, Boston and virtually every city and town in northern and eastern America. Passenger Pigeon was the cheapest meat that could be bought and the squabs were particularly sought after. The gizzards, entrails, blood and even dung were marketed as medical cures for gallstones, stomach-aches, dysentery, colic, infected eyes, fever and epilepsy. Pigeon down and feathers were used for pillows and quilts. There was also a large market for live birds: sportsmen who indulged in trap-shooting bought up perhaps a million birds a year. A shooting club

Passenger Pigeon *Ectopistes migratorius*

might bring in 50,000 birds for a week's competition, nearly all of which would die either by being shot or by having their wings or necks broken by being hurled from the catapult traps. One sporting gentleman could kill more than 500 of these birds in a day's shooting.

After 1860, Pigeon shooting became a full-time occupation for several thousand men. With the advent of the telegraph and the railroad, hunters were easily able to reach the migrating birds wherever they landed and from then on, the nesting grounds were seldom safe. The birds were searched out and the hunters followed them, taking with them hundreds of railway boxcars to fill with their quarry. Local part-time hunters generally used guns, clubs, poles, smudge pots and even fire to kill the birds at nesting sites, while the best professional hunters used huge, specially designed traps and nets. Some of the large nets were baited with decoy birds or 'stool pigeons' – captured birds which had had their eyes sewn up and their legs pinned to a post or 'stool'. Their fluttering wings attracted other Pigeons which the hunters caught in the huge nets, slaughtered and threw into the waiting railway cars. In this way, up to 2,000 birds could be captured at once.

The pressure of the hunters was relentless. By 1878 many of the huge flocks had been destroyed, yet hunters near Petoskey in Michigan descended on a nesting site 50km (30 miles) long and averaging some 8km (5 miles) wide. Their efficiency was astounding. In this one hunt it is estimated that 1,000 million birds were destroyed.

Even this most remarkable and numerous of birds could not withstand forty years of intense market hunting. The great flocks were vanishing. By 1896 there were only 250,000 Passenger Pigeons left. They came together in one last great nesting flock in April of that year outside Bowling Green, Ohio, in the forests on Green River near

Mammoth Cave. The telegraph lines notified the hunters and the railways brought them in from all parts. The result was devastating: 200,000 carcasses were taken, another 40,000 were mutilated and wasted; 100,000 newborn chicks not yet at the squab stage and thus not worth taking were destroyed or abandoned to predators. Perhaps 5,000 birds – all that remained of the species – escaped.

The entire kill of this hunt was loaded into boxcars to be shipped to markets in the east. However, there was a derailment on the line and so the train containing the Passenger Pigeons was shunted into a siding, to wait until the line was cleared. The thousands of dead birds packed tightly into the boxcars soon began to putrefy under the hot sun: eventually the rotting carcasses of all 200,000 birds had to be dumped into a deep ravine a few miles from the railway loading depot.

On 24 March 1900 in Pike County, Ohio, the last Passenger Pigeon seen in the wild was shot dead by a young boy. On 1 September 1914 in the Cincinnati Zoo, Martha – a Passenger Pigeon born in captivity – died at twenty-nine years of age. She was the last of her species.

And so the impossible task had been achieved. But the Passenger Pigeon was not the only victim of ruthless exploitation of market hunters. Scores of bird species were decimated. Many of these paid the ultimate price of extinction. Among them were the now vanished Eskimo Curlew, Labrador Duck, Heath Hen, Painted Vulture and Guadalupe Hawk.

By a sad and remarkable coincidence, just two weeks after Martha – the world's last Passenger Pigeon – died, the Cincinnati Zoo suffered another historic casualty. Not fifteen metres away from Martha's cage was the cage of a Carolina Parakeet (*Conuropsis carolinensis*). When that bird perished, it too proved to be the last of its kind on the planet.

The Carolina Parakeet was a relatively small parrot which measured only 30cm (12in) long from its little yellow beak to its long, pointed tail-tip and weighed in at about 280g (10oz). It was the only parrot native to the United States and, until the later part of the nineteenth century, was an extremely common sight in the eastern deciduous forests, especially around the more densely forested river valleys. It was a bright and colourful bird with a green and yellow body and an orange and yellow head, with a reddish-orange edge to its wings.

The Carolina Parakeet had a defensive behaviour pattern not uncommon in parrots: if one of the flock was injured or killed then the other members of the flock would noisily hover and swoop around the victim, intending to distract the predator and drive it away. Whilst this might have been an extremely effective technique when used against certain natural enemies, when used against men with guns it was disastrous. Hunters would frequently destroy entire flocks after bringing down a single bird. They had many reasons for hunting the Parakeet. Because of its small size and bright colouration, it was extremely popular as a caged pet. Its feathers were much in demand for trimmings, and as the forests were cleared to make way for farming, so its habitat grew smaller, forcing it out to eat seeds, fruit and grain and thus making it very unpopular with the farming population.

By the 1880s it was obvious that the Carolina Parakeet was in danger of extinction, but nothing was done to save it. In the east, the last wild specimen was collected in 1901; the last confirmed sighting was in 1904. A few unauthenticated sightings were later reported but none proven. The bird which was to die in the Cincinnati Zoo in 1914 was the last of its species.

*

The vast migrating flocks of birds of the New World were not limited to the flying variety. There were also a multitude of swimming birds that gathered in huge congregations on islands and in the seas. The most remarkable of these was the Greak Auk (*Alca impennis*).

Again it was a bird that seemed to exist in impossibly vast flocks until man intervened. These birds were, in fact, the original penguins (a word that means 'white head' in Welsh). The now more familiar penguins which only exist in the southern hemisphere were so named because of their resemblance to the Great Auks of the North Atlantic.

The Great Auks were white-breasted and black-backed with wedge-shaped beaks and had streamlined bodies. Agile in the water, where they dived and hunted, on land they were clumsy and awkward. Unable to fly, they shuffled and hopped around, nesting among the rocks that covered the islands they lived on – small islands off the Newfoundland coast, on the Magdalens in the Gulf of St Lawrence, on some islands off the tip of Nova Scotia and in Massachusetts Bay, and in smaller numbers off the Icelandic coast.

Around 1760, when the supply of feathers and down for pillows and feather beds was exhausted through the relentless overhunting of breeding ducks along the eastern coast of North America, feather merchants sent crews of men out to the nesting grounds of the Greak Auk. They harvested the feathers and, in doing so, destroyed every colony of the bird that they found. By 1810, Funk Island, off the Newfoundland coast, had the only West Atlantic colony of Great Auks left. The crews returned to the island each spring until they had killed every bird.

In Europe the birds lasted a little longer off the Icelandic coast, largely because their destruction was not so well organized; still, the same unrestricted killing and egg-gathering steadily reduced the population. By 1844, they had not been sighted for a decade, yet on 3 June that year three Icelandic fishermen discovered two Great Auks nesting on Eldey Island, off the coast of Iceland. The birds had a single egg in their nest. From an extraordinary account of this encounter, we know that two of the fishermen, Jon Brandsson and Sigourer Isleffson, pursued and clubbed the two adult birds to death, while the third member of their team, Ketil Ketilsson, went to the nest and smashed that last egg with his boot. No one ever saw another Greak Auk alive again.

CHAPTER 3

Endless Herds

Quagga and Blue Buck

In the London of the 1830s there was a brief fashion for a most unusual harness animal in high-society circles. It appeared to be some sort of composite animal: half horse and half zebra. The fashion seems to have been started by one Sheriff Parkins who proudly paraded around London in a carriage drawn by a matched pair of these exotic animals.

These creatures were not cross-bred composite animals at all, but a distinct and unique African species called the Quagga (*Equus quagga*). The Quagga was a wild horse from Southern Africa. Its head and neck carried the distinctive black and white zebra stripes which extended through its stiff, upright, mohawk-like mane, which was described by an early observer as 'curious, appearing as if trimmed by art'. The hindquarters were mottled brown or charcoal in colour with a dark dorsal stripe. It had white legs, belly and tail.

At just over twelve hands high at the shoulder, the Quagga was about the size of an Exmoor pony. In conformation the Quagga was rather more horse-like than the zebra, which tends towards a large-headed, donkey-like build. The Quaggas also had smallish ears and a full, well-developed tail. As a harness animal, the Quaggas proved much more responsive than the zebras, which were, because of their tough, rather insensitive mouths, difficult to control.

The Quagga was the only horse or zebra on the South African plains: it once used to roam in herds over the old Cape Colony veldt and, in lesser numbers, through the Orange Free State. In its natural situation the Quagga showed a pattern of behaviour which is typical of the southern zebras. It was almost always to be found in the company of Wildebeest (White-tailed Gnus) or Hartebeest, and ostriches. It has been suggested that this combination of their various talents (the ostriches' good eyesight, the antelopes' powers of smell and the Quaggas' acute hearing) were used together in a remarkable union of defence against their enemies. Certainly, such a group of animals grazing on the open plains would have had a good chance of detecting the presence of any natural predators. With this 'triple alliance', the Quaggas could be warned

Quagga   *Equus quagga*

well in advance of any approaching hunters; their chief enemy, the lion, probably caught very few healthy adult Quaggas. However, this system of defence had little effect when used against the Boers, who arrived with horses, fire-arms and a form of lariat, which they used for live captures.

The colonizing Boers found the Quagga easy prey. Although they themselves would not eat its flesh they saw nothing wrong in feeding it to their servants, since it was the most abundant and available source of food. The hide of the Quagga proved to be most useful and it was made into sacks for storage and the transportation of foodstuffs and farm produce. The hide was strong, lightweight and durable and the many hides that the Boers did not use could be exported. In both the Cape and to the north by the Orange River, the Boers were reported to be 'as much interested in the hide business as in their general occupation of farming'. The Quaggas were shot in their thousands as the Boers advanced.

As well as being an important source of protein and leather, the Quagga was found to have other useful characteristics. It was an energetic and highly-strung animal which was sometimes used as an odd type of 'guard-dog' by the Boers. They kept Quaggas which had been captured when still quite young, which were therefore relatively tame, in the compounds with their domestic stock at night, knowing that the Quaggas would vigorously raise the alarm should any strangers appear. Also, it was known that the Quaggas would frequently viciously attack and even kill unknown intruders – man or beast.

Although the uncertain temperament of the Quagga was exploited by the Boers in Africa in using the animal as a sentry, this aggressive characteristic foiled the only chance that London Zoo ever had of breeding Quaggas when, in the 1860s, their one stallion beat himself to death against the wall of his enclosure in a terrible fit of rage.

In Africa, the Quagga had an unexpectedly limited habitat. This limitation played an important part in its eventual extinction. By the early nineteenth century its numbers were already drastically reduced. The vast herds of the 1840s could not survive the loss of the huge numbers of animals which the Boers slaughtered. Although there were still large herds of Quaggas to be seen on the veldt in the 1860s, these few herds probably made up the species' entire world population. The last wild Quagga was killed in 1878 and in 1883 the last captive Quagga, a solitary female in Amsterdam Zoo, died.

The savannahs and veldts of Africa supported hundreds of different species of animals like the Quagga which, over many thousands of years, remained relatively undisturbed. When the Europeans arrived, like the first settlers in the Americas, they were astounded by the sight of the seemingly limitless wildlife. The exploitation of this wildlife resource without any regard for conservation evoked the same kind of financially motivated killing frenzy that exterminated the Passenger Pigeon in America.

In Africa the endless herds proved as vulnerable as the infinite flocks of America. The balance of nature was quickly upset, the unique habitats of many of the animals were destroyed almost overnight, and the Quagga was not the only species of herd animal to be totally exterminated by the advancing Europeans. In North Africa, hunters eliminated the once wide-ranging herds of Bubal Hartebeest and the elegant, delicate Rufous Gazelle. Meanwhile in Southern Africa, the Boer hunters who extinguished the Quagga were also responsible for the extinction of the nominate race of Burchell's Zebra and the Cape Red Hartebeest.

Africa's very first animal extinction in historic times was

a unique species whose huge, wandering herds fell to those very same Boer guns. This was the strange 'blue-skinned antelope' of South Africa, known as the Blue Buck, or Blaauwbok (*Hippotragus leucophaeus*).

The Blue Buck was a relation of the Roan and Sable Antelopes and lived only in Zwellendam province of the old Cape Colony. The first settlers in the Cape called this antelope the 'blue goat' because of its curved horns, distinctive blue-grey coat and seasonal beard. 'This is the species,' wrote the English naturalist Pennant in his 1781 *History of Quadrupeds*, 'which, from the form of the horns and the length of the hair, seems to connect the goat and antelope tribes.' The settlers were not overly concerned with the ancestry of the Blue Buck but hunted it indiscriminately, for its handsome coat rather than its meat, which, according to the German, Kolbe, who first described the Blue Buck in 1731, was 'generally given to the dogs'. Many of the highly prized skins were exported to Europe although unfortunately virtually none have survived.

The descriptions of the Blue Buck in the wild that survive were only made when Zwellendam province, their natural habitat in the north-west of the Cape, was already quite highly populated. This would suggest that the antelope was at this stage already reduced in numbers and in retreat. It seems, though, that when left alone, the Blue Buck grazed on the open veldt, either in small herds or quite alone. Towards the end of the eighteenth century when its survival was threatened, the Blue Buck was forced to retreat to live in the narrow valleys between Stellenbosch and Graaf Reinet. Despite this retreat it was not, however, a very shy or nervous animal and it was quite easily stalked and shot.

Despite their dwindling numbers, the 'blue velvet' hides of the Blue Buck remained a popular trade item.

Extinction

They were heavily hunted right up until 1796 when the Blue Buck was believed to be extinct. However, that winter a local resident, Sir John Barrow, reported seeing just half a dozen of the rare antelope in the wooded hills above Soete Melk. Their reappearance was short-lived. Rather than attempt to conserve this breed, it was once more eagerly hunted until, in 1799, the last had been shot, and the skin sent to the Leiden Museum. This time, the Blue Buck really was extinct.

CHAPTER 4

Bounteous Seas

Steller's Sea Cow
and Caribbean Monk Seal

Early in June 1741 two Russian ships, the *St Peter* and the *St Paul*, set sail on a historic voyage of discovery from the Russian port of Petropavlosk. The ships sailed out into the fierce and mysterious waters of the North Pacific. Their voyage into these uncharted waters was the culmination of many years of planning by the visionary expedition leader, the Danish officer Vitus Bering, and the powerful and enlightened Russian Czar, Peter the Great.

Bering wished to set out to discover what land links existed between the land masses of Asia and North America, and open new trade routes for Europe by going east rather than west. The Czar saw the expedition as an opportunity to extend the Russian empire into the Americas. And indeed, it was this very expedition that was destined to make Russia the first European power in the Pacific north-west and resulted in a monopoly for over a century in the enormously valuable fur trade of the region.

Within two weeks of setting sail, a storm separated the two ships, but the *St Peter* – with Bering on board – continued to sail on and, on 16 July, the crew sighted the coastline of Alaska. They landed the same day. However, they were not to stay in Alaska for long. After only a day,

Bering insisted that the crew set sail for home in order that they might soon tell of their findings. His impatience was to prove his downfall: the brief Arctic summer was at an end and the storms of winter were approaching.

The *St Peter* made slow progress through the increasingly rough and icy seas; in October, they were still sailing close to Alaskan land. The crew were tired; all of them were weakened by the rigours of the voyage and many of them were afflicted with scurvy. They pulled ashore for a few days to gather the few vegetables they could find and to take on board supplies of fresh water, then set sail again, still hoping to be able to reach home before the worst of the weather struck. When, on 4 November 1741, they saw land ahead the men celebrated, thinking that they were approaching Siberia. Their joy was short-lived. The land mass was only a large island, isolated in the middle of the stormy sea. Knowing now that they had little hope of reaching Russia before the onset of the severest winter weather, Bering issued an order to land on the island. They would spend the winter here and leave for Russia in the spring, when the sea was calmer. In spite of their longing to return home, the sailors could only agree; many had already died from disease and most of those still alive were too weak to be able to work. They managed to dock the ship and carried the sick men and their belongings on to the island.

The island was rocky and inhospitable, although teeming with previously unknown species of marine mammals and birds. Fortunately, the expedition leader had recognized the importance of this voyage in the chronicles of the natural sciences, and Bering's ship had enlisted the services of a trained naturalist: the German professor Georg Wilhelm Steller. It is from Steller that we gain the first view of this undiscovered region and its wildlife.

Steller was enthralled by the diversity of animal life to

be found there and he thrived on the island. But this was not so of Bering, who was among the most impatient to return home. He was unhappy on the island and when, in late November, the *St Peter* was caught up in a storm which dashed the ship against the rocks and wrecked her, he lost hope of ever leaving. He sickened and quickly died. The island was named after him, even though he had hated the place and had been so miserable there. But of the many new species of animals and birds that were discovered on the island, a good number now bear the name of the man who so enthusiastically catalogued them – Georg Steller.

The island proved to have abundant animal life but among all the sea otters, seals and sea lions the men found few animals whose flesh was good to eat. The numerous birds were also all tried but stocks of the few appetizing species which they found were soon exhausted. The only animal they had not eaten was a great beast which they saw swimming out at sea. This beast was observed in large herds throughout the year, basking in the water and grazing on the seaweed that gathered where the rivers of the island flowed out into the sea.

If you asked the question: 'What would an elephant look like if it wanted to be a fish?' you would probably come up with something very like one of these sea beasts. The animal is now known as Steller's Sea Cow (*Hydrodamalis gigas*), but a more apt and descriptive term might be Sea Elephant. With a maximum weight of over seven tons, it is certainly equal to a full-size African elephant, and curiously it was later determined that it was more closely related to the elephant than to either the whales or the seals. In fact, the Sea Cow's prehistoric land-dwelling ancestor was also the ancestor of all Proboscideans, the order which today is represented only by the elephant.

The Steller's Sea Cows' adaption to water rather

Steller's Sea Cow   *Hydrodamalis gigas*

naturally resulted in their whale-like shape. The Sea Cow belonged to the order Sirenidae, which comprises only three genera: Steller's Sea Cow in the Pacific, the much smaller Manatees of the Atlantic and the Dugongs of the Indian Ocean's estuaries.

Steller's Sea Cows were massive animals, they measured from 6 to 9m (20 to 30ft) in length and weighed up to 6,400kg (14,000lb). Outside the whale family, they dwarfed all other sea mammals. They spent their lives partially submerged. Their huge black backs could be seen as they moved slowly through the water, while their snouts emerged from the water to breathe every few minutes. Their skin was extraordinarily thick and looked like 'the bark of an old oak'; in place of teeth, they had strange horny plates of gums which they used to grind the seaweed that they lived on. They had no back legs or even traces of any pelvic bond: but they did have rather short, stumpy forelimbs which were about 67cm (27in) in length. The outer skin of these forelimbs was much thicker and harder than elsewhere and the ends of them were rather like the hooves of a horse, only more pointed and thus more suitable for digging. Below, the 'hooves' were thickly bristled, like scrubbing brushes. Using these seemingly awkward limbs the Sea Cows swam, crawled easily along the bottom of the ocean, held on to slippery rocks, tore seaweed from the ground and caressed their mates.

So it was that when the sailors of Bering's expedition grew tired of the meat they could catch on the island, they set out to catch these Sea Cows. Four or five men would row out to a basking herd and take with them a large iron hook which was tied to a long rope. The end of the rope was held by the men on the shore. As soon as he was able to, a man at the bow with the hook drove it into the back of one of the animals. The men on the beach immediately started to pull the desperately resisting animal to the shore whilst the man in the boat followed it, all the time beating and spiking the Sea Cow in an effort to tire and weaken it. After much difficulty they had the animal ashore and eagerly butchered it.

The flesh was redder than that of most land mammals and was apparently delicious, being reportedly better than beef. The meat from the younger animals was said to be similar to veal. The flesh was covered with a layer of fat nearly 10cm (4in) thick, which was compared to 'May butter' for its richness and had a fine flavour like that of sweet almond oil. It burned with a clear, odourless, smokeless flame.

The meat was so much enjoyed that it soon became the staple diet of the men on Bering Island. Steller had many chances to observe the hunting of the Sea Cows and from his accounts seems to have rather admired the animals and regretted their slaughter. In one hunt he reported how, when one of their number was caught, the others in the herd would gather round in an attempt to save it. They would surround the captured animal and press down on the rope in an effort to break it. They struck at the hook with their tails and quite often managed to remove it in this way. When all else failed, they would try to overturn the boat by jostling it with their backs.

On another hunt he wrote how one male attempted to save his mate, but when – despite his efforts – she was taken, he followed her up on to the shore although the sailors beat and wounded him. Several times, even after she was dead, he shot up to her on the shore and nuzzled against her body, displaying signs of terrible agitation. For two more days he continued his vigil, until at last her carcass was completely butchered and taken away.

The lives of many men of the Bering expedition were saved by the presence of this great and gentle sea mammal.

Its flesh gave the surviving sailors enough strength to eventually rebuild their wrecked ship and return home. They finally docked in Petropavlosk at the end of August 1742 and proclaimed their many discoveries.

Among those discoveries, of course, was the great Sea Cow and such a fine food source in such a barren Arctic region was soon exploited by the many others who followed Bering's expedition, hunting for furs and whales. The Sea Cows were extensively used to provision ships through the long winters – one specimen could feed thirty-three men for a month. Unfortunately, they were hunted wastefully and without thought to the fact that their habitat was obviously limited to these small islands of the Bering Sea. Furthermore, the hunting proved terribly inefficient: it is estimated that for every one Sea Cow successfully hunted and killed, four others were critically wounded and abandoned.

In 1754 a Russian mining engineer named Jakovleff reported on the appallingly wasteful methods used when hunting the Sea Cows, and also stated that these hunts had already entirely exterminated the mammal on nearby Copper Island. Accounts of the time also betrayed an equally appalling cruelty.

'The harpooner stood in the bow of the boat with the hook in his hand and struck as soon as he was near enough to do so, whereupon the men on shore, grasping the other end of the rope, pulled the desperately resisting animal laboriously towards them. Those in the boat, however, made the animal fast by means of another rope and wore it out with continual blows, until tired and completely motionless, it was attacked with bayonets, knives and other weapons and pulled up on land. Immense slices were cut from the still living animal, but all it did was shake its tail furiously and make such resistance with its forelimbs that big strips of the cuticle were torn off. In addition it breathed heavily, as if sighing. From the wounds in the back the blood spurted upward like a fountain. As long as the head was under water no blood flowed, but as soon as it raised the head to breathe the blood gushed forth anew . . . The old and very large animals were much more easily captured than the calves, because the latter moved about much more vigorously, and were likely to escape, even if the hook remained unbroken, by its tearing through the skin.'

The concerned engineer Jakovleff petitioned the authorities to take measures to protect the animals on Bering Island, for he saw no reason in destroying the only major food source available in this region. No one listened to him and in 1767, just twenty-six years after its discovery, the last known Steller's Sea Cow was slaughtered on Bering Island and the species became extinct.

The example of the Steller's Sea Cow proves what is true of the animals of the air and the land is also true of the seas. Fuelled by greed and short-term profit, men choose to believe in nature's limitless bounty despite all evidence to the contrary. Despite the fact that such behaviour leads to the extermination of species after species, and despite the obvious fact that such exterminations destroy the industries these men live on. The vast colonies of sea otters, fur seals and whales that made the North Pacific so valuable to the early explorers were decimated one by one, until they reached the point of 'commercial' extinction: that is, they became so rare, it was no longer financially viable to hunt them. In some cases, this also brought them to the very edge of biological extinction.

For sea mammals, of course, the slaughter was not limited to the North Pacific. It was a hunt that went on world-wide, particularly since the beginning of the period

of European expansion. Indeed, when Christopher
Columbus made his historic voyages of discovery, the first
New World animal that he recorded on the islet of Alta
Vela, to the south of Hispaniola, was the Caribbean Monk
Seal (*Monachus tropicalis*). Much excited by the dis-
covery of this new seal, Columbus immediately ordered
his crew to slaughter eight of them. It was an inauspicious
beginning.

These were large seals, about 240cm (8ft) long and
180kg (400lb) in weight, and at that time were abundant
throughout the Caribbean. By the late seventeenth century the Caribbean Monk Seal had become the source of a
profitable oil industry. By the eighteenth century, this
exploitation, and the associated fur trade, expanded by
extraordinary degrees.

The Monk Seals form a distinctive subfamily (*Mona-
chinae*) of seals which consist of three widely separated
species living in subtropical waters. The other two species
are the Mediterranean Monk Seal and the Hawaiian Monk
Seal. All three species of Monk Seals were hunted extensively for their beautiful fur throughout the eighteenth
and nineteenth centuries. As a result, the Mediterranean
species today has a population of fewer than 500 with very
little hope for recovery or even survival beyond the end of
this century. The Hawaiian species, which was also reduced to around 500 by 1951, has been more fortunate in
that effective protection measures were enforced and it has
increased in numbers to over 2,000.

For the Caribbean Monk Seal, however, the critical
point had been passed by the end of the nineteenth
century. By 1900 the last known populations of Caribbean
Monk Seals lived on the Triangle Keys, which are a series
of small sandy islets off the Yucatan Peninsula. In 1911, a
gang of fishermen who falsely blamed the seals for the
reduction in the numbers of fish being caught, invaded the

islets and slaughtered all of the remaining 200 seals in this region. This was the last-known breeding colony of the species.

Since 1911 small numbers of seals have been observed, but the last of these reliable sightings seems to be one made in Jamaican waters in 1952. A thorough aerial survey of all possible habitats in 1972 and an expedition in April 1980 failed to find any trace of the Caribbean Monk Seal. After both searches it was concluded that the animal was undoubtedly extinct.

CHAPTER 5

Victims of Fashion

Huia and Warrah

At the turn of this century the Duke of York – the future King George V of Great Britain – made a royal visit to New Zealand, during which he was given a number of unusual gifts. One of these was from a Maori chieftain, who with elaborate ceremony presented the Duke the long, elegant black and white tail feathers of a native bird. The Duke was charmed by this token of obvious goodwill, and promptly stuck the feathers into his hatband. By this one impulsive action the Duke unwittingly condemned an already rare species to extinction.

Those long black and white tail feathers belonged to that unique New Zealand bird, the Huia (*Heteralocha acutirostris*). For centuries, the Huia had been a traditional symbol of rank and authority in Maori civilization. By presenting the feathers to the Duke, the Maori chieftain was paying him a compliment of the highest order. Unfortunately when the Duke wore them, he unwittingly set off an immediate European and colonial fashion for the distinctive feathers. Demand for them quickly grew, whether for single feathers or for those on traditional Maori head-dresses. Stuffed specimens of the birds also became popular items to have in the home.

Suddenly, the feathers and corpses of the Huia could be

sold for high prices; hunters and curio collectors descended, seeking out the birds and hiring Maoris to track
them down. The Maoris had traditionally been careful not
to overhunt the Huia to ensure that the birds would
remain available to them. But now, after several epidemics
of imported diseases and a destructive war with the Europeans, the Maoris were dispirited and forced to accept all
the Europeans offered in order to stay alive. They had
little alternative but to accept payment for the hunting of
the Huia.

Beyond its traditional status and its new-found demand
in fashionable circles, the Huia was notable as one of New
Zealand's most remarkable species. Named after the
sound of its distinctive and loud cry, the Huia was a large,
black bird which measured about 48cm (19in) from beak
to tail-tip. It had a bright orange wattle at the base of its
elegant ivory-coloured beak and the prized tail feathers
were broadly tipped with white, giving the tail its distinctive banded appearance. The Huia nested in hollow
trees, but was usually found hopping around on the
ground or in the lower levels of the dense forest in which it
lived.

The feature which made the Huia so extraordinary
amongst the many remarkable birds of New Zealand was
not its beautiful tail nor its nesting habits. Its uniqueness
lay in the difference between the two sexes. Whilst many
birds show major differences in coloration or plumage
between the male and female, in the Huia the two sexes
were differentiated by their distinctive beak forms. These
differences were not a matter of size or colour, they were
actually structural, and the birds differed so much that
when they were first seen by Europeans, the male and
female were believed to be two separate species.

The female had a long, curved beak like that of a
nectar-feeding bird, whilst the beak of the male was short

Huia   *Heteralocha acutirostris*

and strong, shaped rather like that of a starling. The Huias used their two beak forms to great advantage when feeding in pairs: the male bird would attack decaying trees, chopping up and breaking off the rotten bark in search of insects – primarily the Huhu grub, which was its main foodstuff. The female followed and used her long slim beak to probe for more grubs in the smaller crevices which the male could not explore. These differences obviously allowed co-operative, non-competitive feeding between the sexes. No other bird has been found with such extreme structural differences between the sexes, and scientists are at a loss to explain how the Huia alone could have evolved in such a way.

The famous New Zealand ornithologist Sir Walter Buller – who himself killed large numbers of Huia – wrote that in one month a small hunting party of Maoris secured 646 Huia skins. Such catches were not uncommon. It seems likely that this kind of hunting for the fashion trade wiped out the last viable breeding populations of a species that had already been in decline. The Huia was already rare when the Duke of York was presented with his feathers and the depleted population just could not possibly have withstood the onslaught to come.

Cats, dogs, rats and other predators introduced into New Zealand by Europeans, along with forest destruction, had already drastically weakened the bird population. When the extinction of the Huia was suddenly very near, the government of the time made a few token efforts to save it. However, they continued to encourage the deforestation of the Huia's natural habitat.

There was one further pressure which, although not proven, is likely to have had a considerable effect: disease. On examination, some of the existing museum specimens reveal tiny parasitic African and Asiatic ticks which were probably introduced with the Mynahs that the Europeans brought to the Huia's North Island habitat. It seems highly likely that these ticks carried diseases over to the Huia, and these undoubtedly contributed to its demise.

So it was that, when the royal visitor was presented with those elegant tail feathers, the species' fate was sealed. This new and totally frivolous European demand for feathers resulted in five years of intensive hunting and trapping. For the Huia, this was immediately followed by the eternal oblivion of extinction: the very last Huia was sighted on 28 December 1907.

It may seem ludicrous today that such a short-term and frivolous fashion trend should be allowed to extinguish an entire species, but our history is full of such examples which have resulted in the decimation of animal populations. The high-priced fashion among Yemeni men for rhinoceros horn knife-handles and the ludicrous belief throughout the Far East in the power of powdered rhinoceros horn as a means of increasing male sexual powers have brought all rhinoceros species to the very edge of extinction. Indeed, it was this same absurd belief in the sexually stimulating powers of its spectacular, multi-tined antlers that resulted in the extinction of Schomburgk's Deer, a rare and beautiful swamp-dwelling deer from Thailand, in 1932.

If one were to list absurd fads and fashions that have led to animal extinctions, the case of that giant red deer, the Eastern Elk or Wapiti, deserves a dishonourable mention. Although certainly over-hunted for its meat and hide throughout its range, the cause of its final extinction was a fad among members of the American fraternal lodge of the 'Order of the Elks' for the animal's decorative upper canine teeth as an engraved watch-chain fob.

Above all, however, it is the passing fashions in the feather and fur trades that have led to the most widespread destruction of wildlife. Today, for example, every species of the spotted and striped wild cat is endangered because of the fur trade.

One of the animals which the fur trade fashion took a fatal passing interest in during the late nineteenth century was a rather unusual beast called the Warrah or Antarctic Wolf (*Dusicyon australis*). The Warrah was found on the remote Falkland Islands off the coast of Argentina. There were no human inhabitants on the Falklands at all until Europeans discovered them. Indeed, although there were many sea birds and sea mammals on their shores, the Warrah was the only large animal to roam the interior regions.

Believed by some to be a wolf and by others to be a giant form of fox, the Warrah was neither. It was a unique species which evolved under rather mysterious circumstances. The first description on record came from Richard Simson who sailed on the British ship the *Welfare* and was engaged in an early war for the Falkland Islands in 1690. 'We saw foxes twice as big as in England, we caught a young one, which we kept on board for some months.' However, when the British ship engaged itself in a battle, the Warrah became an early Falkland War casualty. It decided a battleship was no fit place for a beast and leapt overboard.

The Warrah was noted by several other travellers to the Falklands, but it was not until 1833, when its population was already critically depleted, that Charles Darwin wrote about the animal and awakened an interest in it. While on the islands Darwin studied the animal and collected three skins, two of which were later presented to the London Zoological Society.

As Darwin observed, the Warrah measured between 120 and 160cm (4 and 5ft) in length and had a large wolfish head. Its legs were much shorter than those of a true wolf, and it stood only 60cm (2ft) tall at the shoulder. The Warrah's coat was coloured a blend of brown, yellow and black, with black ears and a white belly, and a white-tipped tail like that of a fox. It was apparently fox-like in its living habits, living in earths which it dug for itself, but wolf-like in its hunting methods.

What interested Darwin most about the Warrah was that it was the only predator on the islands and, apart from a small variety of mouse, the only land mammal. The Warrah seemed to live on an unlikely diet of mice, sea birds and eggs. It is also possible that it might have lived on some smaller sea mammals as there are some accounts of the animal actually leaping into the sea in pursuit of prey.

Just how the Warrah could have evolved on these isolated islands without any really substantial prey species, and with no other related species on the islands at all, was something of a mystery to Darwin. It has been suggested that the forebears of the Warrah drifted over to the Falklands on the ice from Patagonia, or perhaps many species once lived in the pre-glacial forests of the Falkland Islands, but that only this Antarctic Wolf was able to survive. Whatever the reason, it is a mystery not now likely to be resolved.

Early sheep and cattle farmers on the Falklands rather predictably killed or trapped the Warrah whenever they could, but as news of this unusual animal spread, something of a foreign market developed. Some animals were taken alive for zoos, others were killed so that their skins could be preserved for a collectors' market and natural history museums, but most were exported for the fur trade.

By 1839 the Warrah was already rare and the law of supply and demand resulted in pelt prices rapidly increasing. Soon after Darwin left the Falkland Islands, the colonial government set a bounty on the animals. Hunters moved in on the already greatly reduced population, eager to catch the animal both for the bounty and for the pelt. The Warrah was given a largely undeserved reputation as a fierce predator, which served well as a justification for more killing. The shepherds who lived on the Falkland Islands regarded it as a dangerous pest and gladly took every opportunity to kill it.

Interestingly, in 1868 one emaciated live specimen actually reached England and was sent off to London Zoo, where it survived alone for several years. This Warrah had been, along with three small birds, the only animal to survive the long sea journey from the Falklands to England. Hundreds of other animals and birds had also been shipped, but died on the journey as a result of criminally careless shipping arrangements. The man who had arranged the appalling transportation of the animals was a Mr Lecomte, a man who was also responsible for wiping out the Falkland Islands' entire King Penguin population. Through a large-scale live capture programme in which he supplied King Penguins to Europe, he managed to eliminate the entire King Penguin colony.

The last straw for the Warrah came when for a brief time it became the object of a suddenly fashionable demand in New York. The Astor family furriers in New York became interested in this mysterious wolf-fox with the luxurious coat. They hired their own hunters on the Falkland Islands. It was a highly successful expedition: a ship loaded with skins sailed back to New York, and the Astor fur merchants converted these into rather sumptuous fur coats of the 'Antarctic Wolf-Fox' or 'Falkland Island Aquara Dog', as they were sometimes called. The store then proudly advertised the sale of the coats as a 'last opportunity sale'. This was literally quite true, for as Mr Astor himself acknowledged, his 'hunters had nearly extirpated the species'. Indeed, the last Warrah was shot and skinned at Shallow Bay in the Hill Cove Canyon in 1876.

CHAPTER 6

In the Name of Science

Ivory-billed Woodpecker
and Dwarf Caribou

Beyond the demands of commercial fashion markets in
such areas as the fur and feather trades, there has
been considerable destruction of a number of rare animal
species by what may seem a most unlikely faction: the
scientific community itself. Remarkably, natural history
museums and their collectors during the past couple of
centuries have played a fatal role in the extinction of a
number of animal species.

The present predicament of the Californian Condor as a
critically endangered bird was predetermined by the fact
that the museums of the world were paying large sums of
money for specimens. Between 1880 and 1910, 288 Condors were killed for museum collections, and several
hundred eggs were stolen. By 1910 there were less than
sixty Californian Condors left in the world. In 1989 there
were twenty-seven captive birds left alive and none in the
wild at all.

Museum and private collecting of animal specimens
generally has little or no effect on species with large
populations, but unfortunately the species which are in
greatest demand by collectors are those which are least
able to sustain population losses. It is precisely because a
species is known to be rare that collectors pursue many

animals. (Indeed, this is also true in the fur trade as well. Many conservationists note that the usual effect of listing a species as endangered is an immediate doubling of its market value. This inevitably results in a sharp increase in slaughter and a further collapse in population.)

As we have already noted in Chapter Three, the African continent's first man-caused extinction in historic times was that unique species of antelope called the Blue Buck, and the last half dozen of these animals were hunted down and killed by collectors for a German museum in 1799.

Similar stories are told of a number of bird species that have been hunted down to the very last specimen by men who behaved like mad collectors obsessed with gaining infamy as the one who finally eliminated the species. One can cite numerous cases from the colourful Guadalupe Flicker to the Koreke or New Zealand Quail – the last twenty of which have the distinction of being bagged in a single afternoon in 1868 by that nation's most famous ornithologist, Sir Walter Buller.

One of the most outrageous examples is that of one of America's most prized and well-known bird species, the Ivory-billed Woodpecker. America's naturalist James Audubon called the Ivory-billed Woodpecker (*Campephilus principalis principalis*), the 'Van Dyke' of American birds. A bird as rare as it was beautiful, it was precisely because of these factors that it became the preferred species for museum collections, which, when historic records are examined, have proved to be the main cause of the bird's extinction.

The Woodpeckers are among the most striking and most widespread of the world's birds. The second largest and certainly the most famous of all the Woodpeckers was the American Ivory-billed Woodpecker. (The largest – by about 5cm or 2in – was the lesser-known Imperial

Ivory-billed Woodpecker *Campephilus principalis principalis*

Woodpecker of Mexico, now also believed to be extinct.) It was a large, beautiful bird about 50cm (20in) long, covered with glossy, blue-black feathers which were patterned with strong, distinctive white markings. On its head it carried a glowing red crest and also the feature which gave this Woodpecker its name – a strong, 8cm (3in) long, ivory-coloured bill, which it used to chop the bark away from dead trees so that it could reach the grubs which lived beneath.

The Ivory-billed Woodpecker needed considerable tracts of mature timberland to be able to find sufficient food to live on, feeding as it did on the insects which live under the bark of newly dead trees; each breeding pair would cover a territory of more than 2,000 acres. With their conspicuous markings and loud, resonant calls these large birds were once relatively easy to find in their vast woodland habitats. However, destruction of mature timberland during the last century has been almost total apart from a few pockets and the birds have suffered accordingly.

Although by 1900 the Ivory-bill was even rarer than the Californian Condor, a great deal is known about the bird. It was evidently never a common bird. Despite its small numbers, its territory was broad, if specialized and thinly populated. Before the heyday of the timber industry in the American South (1800 to 1900) the Ivory-bill inhabited virtually all mature low-lying timberland in south-eastern North America. Its crest and beak were valued items of Indian trade. In 1939 a beak was found in an Indian grave as far north-west as Colorado. Mark Catesby, in his *Natural History of Carolina* (1731), wrote: 'The bills of these birds are much valued by the Canada Indians, who make coronets of them for their Princes and great warriors.'

James T. Tanner's classic 1942 study (sponsored by the

National Audubon Society) gives us extensive knowledge of the range, habits and needs of the Ivory-bill. The strength and vigour of these birds often astonished even the most knowledgeable ornithologists. Alexander Wilson wrote of one he wounded and kept in his hotel room in Wilmington, North Carolina: 'In less than an hour I returned and, on opening my door, he set up a distressing shout, which appeared to proceed from grief that he had been discovered in his attempts to escape. He had mounted along the side of the window, nearly as high as the ceiling, a little below which he began to break through. The bed was covered with large pieces of plaster, the lath was exposed and a hole large enough to admit the fist, opened to the weatherboards; so that, in less than another hour he would certainly have succeeded in making his way through.'

The Ivory-bill became the most sought-after and investigated of all rare birds. Once its rarity was fully realized, instead of attempting to instigate preservation programmes, museums clamoured for specimens. Indeed, it seemed that they were in competition to see who could secure the highest number of Ivory-billed Woodpeckers before they became extinct. Every major museum seems to have managed to acquire a considerable quota of them.

It has been estimated that the maximum number of Ivory-bills which existed at any one time in America could only have been about three hundred – yet today there are over four hundred traceable specimens of the Ivory-billed Woodpeckers, with one hundred and forty of them in just two American museums alone. By any standards this should have been totally unacceptable behaviour by institutions and individuals who knew only too well that the species was headed for extinction.

By 1939, Tanner estimated there could be no more than

twenty-two surviving Ivory-bills in the United States. He did not base his figures on sightings, but instead calculated the theoretical capacity of any breeding areas that were still intact. The real population might very well have been even lower. The last generally accepted sighting of the American Ivory-billed Woodpecker was in 1951, and although there have been rumours of sightings, it seems certain the American race is now extinct. The only hope for the entire species is with its only cousin, the Cuban Ivory-billed Woodpecker (*Campephilus principalis bairdii*). However, the picture with the Cuban bird is not all that much brighter.

By 1960, there were believed to be fewer than twenty Cuban birds, and in 1970 this was believed to have fallen to twelve. After 1974, no Cuban Ivory-billed Woodpeckers were sighted at all and it was believed that this bird too had become extinct.

Then, remarkably, in March 1986, Cuban ornithologists sighted a pair of Ivory-bills. Within a year three more birds were sighted and the Cuban government ordered an immediate end to logging in this region near the Jaguani Forest Reserve. And so, for the time being, the Cuban Ivory-billed Woodpecker survives, but only as one of the rarest of all the planet's species.

Perhaps one of the most bizarre of all these extinctions 'in the name of science' was the case of Canada's Dwarf Caribou. This dwarf form of reindeer, most often called Dawson's Caribou (*Rangifer dawsoni*), became extinct as a result of an academic debate.

Dawson's Dwarf Caribou lived on Queen Charlotte Islands, Canada's most westerly outpost, just below the Alaska panhandle. This Caribou was a very small, pale, possibly relic subspecies which had evolved in a unique habitat. All other Caribou species ranged the dry interior of the north and the land area of the Arctic region. By contrast, the home of these small Caribou – the swamp barrens (muskeg) of the Queen Charlottes where the only firm land is wooded and the humidity often rises to phenomenal levels – seems remarkably unsuitable.

The Haida Indians, who inhabited the islands for at least five thousand years before the Europeans came along, did not know about the Caribou even by tradition. The Haida seldom ventured into the densely forested interior of the islands, where the Caribou lived, until the white market for furs opened up. And even then, the Haida stuck close to the river banks to set their traps for bear, otter and marten.

The Dwarf Caribou, despite their reclusive habits, were occasionally seen and shot for meat. Rumours of their existence spread to the mainland. The first published mention of the Caribou is in G. M. Dawson's first report on the islands in 1878, when he wrote that there was good evidence for the existence of Wapiti (or North American Elk) in the northern part of Graham Island – the largest of the Queen Charlotte Islands. He later corrected the 'Wapiti' to 'Caribou'. The scientific community became alerted and demanded some physical proof of its existence.

In 1880 Alexander Mackenzie, a trader for the Hudson's Bay Company in Old Masset, offered a reward to any native who brought him in a specimen of this elusive animal. A Haida named Elthkeega, out hunting with his bear dogs, drove a cow and a bull Caribou into Virago Sound and killed them there. He took the bull to Mackenzie and claimed his reward. A fragment of the skull of this bull Caribou, still with one antler attached, eventually found its way to the Provincial Museum in Victoria and there was examined by Ernest Thompson Seton in 1900. After careful consideration, this famous pioneering naturalist and author announced that this skull came from a completely new species and gave it its present Latin name.

The skull and Seton's analysis were not, however, accepted as conclusive. In fact, they seem to have just fuelled a debate over the possibility of any species of Caribou surviving in such a habitat. Notable objectors were the naturalist-missionaries Collinson and Keen, who doubted his opinion and dismissed the evidence as fraudulent.

They believed that the Haida had brought the specimen down from Alaska simply in order to claim the reward. But another missionary, the Revd Charles Harrison, who was a fluent Haida speaker and claimed to have actually eaten the dried meat of the animal, was far less sceptical about the natives' stories. In fact, after initial interest had been aroused, several Haida came to tell him of sightings in Virago Sound near the ruined village of Kung.

In March 1901, a year after Seton had named the animal, Harrison spent ten days in the woods along the Sound accompanied by five Haidas and Revd Collinson's son. They found abundant tracks and dung and retrieved some Caribou hair. A year later, another party saw more tracks and brought back a Caribou horn. Revd Harrison concluded that the animal undoubtedly did exist but that its range was very limited, extending only through the areas of Graham Island north of latitude 54° and bordering Virago Sound.

With the evidence of its existence mounting, interest in the Caribou increased. It was quite obvious that the elusive animals were extremely rare, but rather than organizing some attempt at live capture or a programme of protection, the scientific community responded by offering ever larger rewards for hunters to track down specimens for museum collections. Hunters and naturalists came from considerable distances to search for these animals throughout their small, known territory.

On 1 November 1908, two men were hunting in a large swamp barren inland from Virago Sound. They saw a small herd of four Dwarf Caribou near the centre of the barren and, as they drew nearer, they identified them as two bull Caribou with horns, a cow and a calf. The animals seemed to show no fear of the hunters at all but simply stood quite still while, one after another, they fell to the guns.

The debate among the academics had now been resolved to the satisfaction of the scientific community. Because they now had sufficient physical evidence, it was agreed that the mysterious Dawson's Dwarf Caribou did in fact exist – or, more properly, had existed up to the point at which the hunters opened fire. For as it was later found, this little gathering proved to be the last herd in existence.

When the hunters slaughtered these animals in order to collect the reward the scientific community had put on their heads, they succeeded in wiping out the species. Dawson's Dwarf Caribou were far rarer than anybody had ever imagined. There is no record of anybody ever seeing one of these shy, reclusive animals again. Victims of a rather trivial academic debate, confirmation of the existence and the extinction of Dawson's Dwarf Caribou was reached at exactly the same apocalyptic moment.

CHAPTER 7

Careless Losses

Stephen Island Wren and Hawaiian Honeycreepers

At the northern tip of New Zealand's South Island, two miles from the spectacularly mountainous D'Urville Island in Cook Strait, is Stephen Island. This tiny wooded island, which measures no more than 2.6 sq. km (1 sq. mile) in size, but rises abruptly from the sea to a height of 300m (1,000ft) was the sole habitat for one of the world's smallest and rarest birds: the Stephen Island Wren (*Xenicus lyalli*).

The four distinct 'wren' species of New Zealand are not actually related to true wrens at all. They are an eccentric family of birds (*Acanthisittidae*) that have evolved separately from the Wren family, but have developed a similar appearance and behaviour pattern. The Stephen Island Wren was a mottled brown colour with a yellow-green belly and throat. It was semi-nocturnal in habit and hid in holes in the rocks, running like a mouse across the ground rather than resorting to flight.

The man who discovered the Stephen Island Wren was a Mr Henry Travers, who in 1894 was appointed lighthouse keeper on the uninhabited island. Unfortunately, for company in this lonely job, Mr Travers brought with him a pet cat. Indeed, it was the cat who brought the birds to the attention of Travers, routinely catching

AUGUSTANA LIBRARY
UNIVERSITY OF ALBERTA

them and laying them dead at the lighthouse keeper's feet.

When Henry Travers eventually sent a few of the tiny birds to a noted ornithologist, the man wrote back in great excitement stating that this was an as yet undiscovered and unique species. As soon as he could, the ornithologist intended to come to Travers on the island. Shortly thereafter, Travers wrote an apologetic letter to the ornithologist. The expert's trip, Travers said, would be a wasted one. Since last writing, the lighthouse keeper had searched the island high and low, and it appeared that the pet cat had hunted down and killed the entire species! Sad to say, this was so. No one ever saw another Stephen Island Wren again.

Fortunately, few creatures have had such a sudden and dramatic entry and exit from the annals of natural history, but the simultaneous discovery and extermination of the Stephen Island Wren does demonstrate just how easily the balance of nature can be upset by human intervention, particularly when it comes to the careless introduction of alien species. This is especially true with rather fragile tropical island habitats.

New Zealand, along with many of the Pacific and Indian Ocean Islands, had no native mammals (aside from bats), and no predators at all. Consequently, invading humans with their accompanying cats, dogs and rats proved a disaster – especially to the nearly tame, ground-nesting birds. Europeans also brought with them pigs, goats, cattle, rabbits, mongooses, monkeys, deer and many other species that, if they did not prey directly on the native animals, usually destroyed the habitat so dramatically that life became impossible for them. Indeed, many a lush tropical island where Europeans left pigs, goats, rats and rabbits changed in a couple of decades into desert islands that were unable to support any life at all.

Cats, rats and mongooses are among the most disastrous of introduced predators in island habitats so far as the native species are concerned, while pigs, goats and rabbits are the most successful in actually destroying the vegetable habitat itself. Species introduced by Europeans have resulted in the extinction of at least a dozen species of those long-legged walking birds called Rails, and an equal number of flying but ground-nesting bird species on South Pacific and Indian Ocean Islands. In the West Indies over a dozen species of large fruit- and seed-eating rodents called Quemis, Hutias, Isolobodons and Agoutis became extinct. These gentle, harmless animals were about the size and shape of beavers, but proved no competition for the ferocious new carnivores that invaded their islands.

Nor were animals in the land and air the only victims of introduced species; at least half a dozen species of fish have become extinct through humans introducing exotic new species into lakes and rivers. Some of these were intentional. The introduction of the Rainbow Trout resulted in the extinction of the native New Zealand Grayling (*Prototroctes oxyrhynchus*) in 1923. Others were accidental: sea-going Lamprey introduced through the newly opened St Lawrence Seaway into the American Great Lakes resulted in the final decline and extinction of their famous Jumbo Herring – the Blackfin (*Coregonus nigripinnus*) and Deepwater (*Coregonus johannae*) Ciscos – by 1960.

Possibly some of the best places to study the disastrous results of carelessly introduced exotic species on native animals are the Hawaiian Islands. Here we can see, particularly in the cases of the many now-extinct Hawaiian

Honeycreeper (*Drepanididae*) and Hawaiian Honeyeater (*Meliphagidae*) birds, the tragic chain-reactions these introductions cause.

These beautiful, isolated islands in the middle of the Pacific Ocean are made of lava and coral limestone which, when combined with the subtropical temperatures and phenomenal rainfall typical of the region, gave rise to one of the most unique and diverse natural collections of flora and fauna to be found anywhere on the planet. Dense and varied rainforest, expanses of parkland and huge ravine areas – wherein no less than 97 per cent of plant and tree species were unique to the islands.

But by the 1950s, three-quarters of this rich natural forest was already lost to cultivation, cattle-browsing and fire. If the islands were to lose much more of their forest cover, they would lose their watersheds too and rapidly erode into nothing more than a wasteland, unable to support anything more than the most basic life forms. Already, at least 270 Hawaiian plant species, subspecies or varieties are completely extinct and another 800 are seriously endangered.

At least four tree species which were unique to the islands are now either extinct or survive only as single specimens. The life cycle of each of these trees (Pritchard Palms and Hibiscadelphi) was vitally bound up – probably symbiotically – with the lives of certain birds, which are also now extinct. Among this list of extinct birds, which once lived in such a close relationship with the trees, are many of the different forms of Honeycreepers, a family of birds entirely endemic to the Hawaiian Islands.

The Hawaiian Honeycreepers are considered the youngest of all bird families and are among the most beautiful and varied of birds. It is believed that all Hawaiian Honeycreepers are descended from one ancestor species. It is therefore astonishing that, one hundred years ago, the Hawaiian Honeycreepers had evolved from this one form into nine genera, twenty-two species and sixty-four subspecies.

The Honeycreepers varied in length from 10 to 21.5cm (4 to 8.5in). All are, or were, extremely beautiful and often brilliant birds, demonstrating extreme diversity in structure – especially in their bill shapes – with each different form adapting a shape to suit its specific habits.

Hawaiian Honeyeater: Oahu O-O   *Moho apicalis* (above)
Hawaiian Honeycreeper: Mamo   *Drepanis pacifica* (below)

Most of the different forms evolved around the abundant flowering trees which were once such a distinctive feature of the Hawaiian forests, adapting to feed on the wide variety of different foods that the trees provided, including seeds, nuts, fruits, nectar, caterpillars and many insects. As so often happens with island birds, the specialization that allowed them to survive in such large numbers in such a limited space proved to be a weakness when new forces or competitors intruded. The more highly specialized Honeycreepers were the most vulnerable, whilst the varieties of Honeycreepers which covered the widest ranges and lacked significant regional variations have survived the best: however, 40 per cent of all Honeycreeper species have already become extinct and a further 40 per cent are today in immediate danger of the same fate.

With their varied and beautiful plumage, certain varieties of the Honeycreeper were often much sought after by collectors, especially as their rarity became more and more apparent. The spectacular Mamo had always been hunted for its black and yellow plumage which was an essential part of the royal Hawaiian cloaks. When European firearms were made available, this bird was rapidly hunted into extinction. The pressure put upon the birds by hunters and specimen collectors was, however, a relatively small factor in the birds' disappearance.

The first and most obvious cause of their decline was the destruction of the native forests. Less than a quarter of the original Hawaiian forests survive today as the lowlands have given way to cultivation and the mountains play host to introduced goats, cattle, pigs and deer. As cattle grazed on and consequently destroyed the forests, the Honeycreepers retreated: the birds were forced to live in smaller and smaller areas, in denser populations than ever before. Competition for food became fierce and under these relatively crowded conditions, pests and diseases spread more rapidly.

When new parasites arrived in Hawaii on the backs of imported birds, the Honeycreepers quickly became affected. As early as the 1890s, the Honeycreepers of Kauai were seen to be affected by strange new diseases: specimens were taken and found to be infested with worms and tapeworms. 'Bumblefoot', or Bird Pox, came in with chickens and many Honeycreepers were observed with its symptoms. However, one particular type of introduced bird was to play a far more indirect but sinister role than this in the decline of the Honeycreeper.

Before the year 1826, no mosquitoes lived on the Hawaiian Islands. In that year, the Night Mosquito arrived on the island of Maui as a ship's stowaway. The Night Mosquito found the subtropical atmosphere of the rainforests much to its liking and rapidly spread throughout the islands. When domestic pigeons were introduced to Hawaii, they too rapidly spread through the islands and it was the arrival of these two different organisms that marked the end of many of the Honeycreepers.

The reason for this was that many of the domestic pigeons were infected with avian malaria, and when the mosquitoes fed on the pigeons, they picked up the infection and carried it to the Honeycreepers, who were by now living in crowded colonies in restricted areas of the islands and were therefore a perfect target for the disease. With no chance to develop any resistance to the new disease, the Honeycreepers died by the thousands. The only varieties to be spared were the Honeycreepers which lived permanently up in the mountains, as the mosquitoes could not survive above altitudes of more than about 600m (2,000ft).

The extinct Honeycreepers include: Mamo (*Drepanis pacifica*), Black Mamo (*Drepanis funerea*), Ula-Ai-

Hawane (*Ciridops anna*), Laysan Apapane (*Himatione sanguinea freethi*), Great Amakihi (*Loxops sagittirostris*), Molokai Alauwahio (*Loxops maculata flammea*), Lanai Alauwahio (*Loxops maculata montana*), Oahu Akepa (*Loxops coccinea rufa*), Hawaiian Akiola (*Hemignathus obscurus obscurus*), Lanai Akiola (*Hemignathus obscurus lanaiesis*), Oahu Akiola (*Hemignathus obscurus ellisianus*), Kauai Akiola (*Hemignathus obscurus procerus*), Oahu Nukupuu (*Hemignathus lucidus lucidus*), Kauai Nukupuu (*Hemignathus lucidus hanapepe*), Maui Nukupuu (*Hemignathus lucidus affinis*), Greater Koa Finch (*Psittirostra palmeri*), Lesser Koa Finch (*Psittirostra flaviceps*) and Kona Finch (*Psittirostra kona*).

Tragically, the Hawaiian Honeyeaters suffered similarly from the consequences of European colonization. The extinct Honeyeaters include: Kioea (*Chaetoptila angustipluma*), Oahu O-O (*Moho apicalis*), Molokai O-O (*Moho bishopi*).

These wonderfully adapted and beautiful tropical birds, so well-suited to their island paradise, now prove to be a classic example of how disastrous and often unpredictable chain-reactions can result from human interference with the natural balance of a fragile environment.

CHAPTER 8

The Trophy Hunters

Golden Lion and Bali Tiger

The big-game trophy hunter does not hunt for food or
profit. Indeed, the tracking down and shooting of a
target animal usually costs him a great deal of money. He
kills simply for the pleasure of it. These are the hunters
who call themselves 'sportsmen' and kill animals simply to
take their head or skin as a souvenir of the hunt.

Despite considerable disapproval of this activity in
recent times in the West, there is still a world-wide,
multi-million dollar illegal industry catering to wealthy
trophy hunters who wish to hunt rare and endangered
species. Unscrupulous guides commonly bribe guards
and officials on behalf of the trophy hunter to gain entry
into many government parks and reserves in order to
slaughter rare species. It happens even today, not only in
Africa and South America, but in every country with
substantial game preserves in North America, Europe and
Asia.

Perhaps the most sought-after big game animals are the
big cats, particularly the lions and tigers. These are
considered the 'noblest' of trophies, as they are among the
few who are capable of actually fighting back to some
degree.

The two largest animals of the lion family were the

Barbary Golden Lion (*Panthera leo leo*) of North Africa
and the Cape Black-maned Lion (*Panthera leo mela-
nochaitus*) of South Africa. Partly because they were
the largest and most desirable trophy species, and partly
because they lived in regions most accessible to
Europeans, these two subspecies were successfully
exterminated by the big-game hunters.

The Barbary Golden Lion, like the Cape Black-maned
Lion, was a huge animal reaching weights of 227kg
(500lb) and lengths of 3m (10ft) from nose to tail. The
Barbary Golden Lion was particularly distinguished by its
great golden mane, which was larger than any other
subspecies', extending along to the middle of the back and
most of the belly as well. As its name implied, the Cape
Black-maned Lion was notable for its distinctive black
mane, which was second only to the Barbary Lion's mane
in size.

The Cape Black-maned Lion was the first to go. It was
hunted to extinction by the same ruthless English and
Afrikaans marksmen who extinguished the Blue Buck and
the Quagga. The last Cape Black-maned Lion was shot by
a General Bisset in Natal in 1865.

The Golden Lion, although hunted since the days of
the ancient Romans, lingered somewhat longer in the
Atlas Mountains of North Africa. Its territory diminished
with the rapid improvement of firearms in the late
nineteenth century in the hands of French and Arab
sportsmen. The last true Barbary Golden Lion was
reported killed in the Atlas Mountains in 1922.

Although the lion is considered to be 'King of the Beasts',
it is not the largest of the great cats. The tiger has that
distinction, and unfortunately it is a distinction which
makes it the most popular species of all so far as trophy
hunters are concerned.

In 1900 there was already a considerable depletion of the tigers' range and numbers. However, as recently as 1930 there had been no tiger extinctions and the wild population numbered about 100,000. Since that time, the fashion for tiger trophies and the market for tiger skins has taken its toll. By 1972, tigers had completely disappeared from the greater part of their territory throughout Asia and their total population was estimated to be only 5,000 animals.

Today, of the eight subspecies of tiger, three are extinct and four are severely endangered. Whilst deforestation and the destruction of the wild game on which the tiger feeds can be blamed for some of the losses, the tigers' decline can be attributed for the most part to the poachers who hunt the animal for the fur and trophies.

Up to the turn of the century, tigers were found throughout Asia with each subspecies or race within its region adapting in size and habits to the demands of its own particular environment. They were highly effective predators. Unlike lions, tigers are solitary animals, coming together only to mate, preferring to live and hunt alone. They search for food at dusk or by night and keep to the more densely covered areas. They are less frequent, more economical killers than most predators, hiding their kill and returning to it several times until it is finished.

Tigers are also highly adaptable. The tigers' size and strength make mammals as large as the water buffalo their natural prey, yet their speed and agility allow them to snatch small birds out of the air.

Tigers range considerably in size from region to region. The largest species were the Siberian and Caspian Tigers (*Panthera tigris virgata*) which weighed up to 320kg (770lb), and measured over 3m (10ft) in body length – without the tail. The smallest Tigers were the Bali and the Javan (*Panthera tigris balica*) races, both of which had length measurements half of that of the larger species at 1.5m (5ft) and weight of about one-fifth of the larger races.

Unfortunately, it appears that these tigers at either extreme of the size scale (as well as the extreme north and south of their geographic range) have proved the most vulnerable to human predation. The Bali, Caspian and Javan Tigers are all now extinct, and the Siberian race is critically endangered.

The Bali Tiger was once a fairly common beast. In 1912 Ernst Schwarg described it as similar to the small Javan Tiger, but even smaller still. It shared the Javan Tiger's short, dense hair but the ground colour of its fur was brighter and the light markings a clearer white. Of all the tigers, it had the brightest and most clearly marked coat. Its numbers declined sharply between the two world wars when the local people acquired firearms and joined with the Dutch colonials to organize frequent, fashionable tigerhunts. By the mid-1930s, a survey of the Dutch Indies for the International Wildlife Protection Commission revealed of the tigers that: 'A few yet live in West Bali but they are having a hard time because they are much sought after by hunters from Java, so they will certainly disappear within a few years. The species also exists in north-west and south-west Bali.'

The tiger disappeared very quickly indeed and not just from the western parts of Bali, where the Commission saw the most danger for it, but from the whole country. The last known Bali Tiger was a female which was shot at Sumbar Kima, West Bali, on 27 September 1937.

The story of the huge Caspian Tiger was similar. Uncontrolled hunting in the Caspian region of the USSR, Iran and Afghanistan so depleted the population that by 1970 there were only a dozen left in the mountains of

Bali Tiger   *Panthera tigris balica*

northern Iran. By 1980, these too appeared to have gone.

The Javan Tiger survived only a little longer than his cousins, but by 1971, there were fewer than twelve animals in south-eastern Java. By 1981, despite attempts to set up a reserve, only two were believed to survive. By 1988, this last couple of persecuted animals had vanished, and the Javan Tiger became the third race to become extinct this century.

An international survey in 1972 revealed the tiger was in real trouble in all its habitats. As we have seen, it was already too late for the extinct Bali and soon-to-be extinct Caspian and Javan races. The Siberian, Chinese and Sumatran races were down to between two and three hundred animals each. Information on the Indo-Chinese race was incomplete, but it was thought that its population was about one thousand. Only the nominate race, the Bengal or Indian Tiger, survived in substantial numbers. It was believed to have a population in excess of two thousand, but due to the popularity of hunting, this too was dwindling quickly. Indeed, in the same year as the survey, one maharaja boasted that he alone had been responsible for the deaths of more than one thousand Bengal Tigers.

Something had to be done, and done quickly. The last of the tiger populations could not survive for much longer. The World Wildlife Fund, largely inspired by the efforts of Guy Mountford, launched the Save the Tiger appeal in 1972. It was WWF's largest project up to that time and required careful negotiations in order to win the co-operation of several national governments.

It was recognized that extensive popular fund raising would be required if the operation was to achieve any long-term effect. The WWF proved equal to the task of raising several million dollars in donations, as well as achieving comparable grants from the various governments. The organizers were fully aware that time was of the essence and that the tiger populations were spiralling rapidly downwards in all its territories.

Logically enough, the bulk of the rescue effort went into its work on the Indian subcontinent, where the chances of success seemed most likely. And true enough, the project workers were soon rewarded by remarkable results in a relatively short time.

With essential local and national government involvement, a score of large reserves covering over 20,500 sq. km (8,000 sq. miles) have been established in a score of reserves, and the Indian Tiger population has doubled to about 4,000. Elsewhere, encouragement and aid from the World Wildlife Fund's Save the Tiger initiative has heightened international awareness of the problem. The population of the Siberian Tiger has increased to 500, and Chinese populations to 250 or more. The Sumatra population now appears to be around 500, while the Indo-Chinese race may be around 2,000 – despite extensive and ongoing poaching operations.

It is tragic that three races of tiger are now extinct, and the fate of the Siberian, Chinese and Sumatran races is by no means totally secure, but with continued vigilance the tiger now seems certain to survive – in at least a couple of its forms – for some time to come.

CHAPTER 9

The Bounty Hunters

Thylacine and
Mexican Silver Grizzly

The Thylacine, or Tasmanian Pouched Wolf (*Thylacinus cynocephalus*), was without any doubt the strangest 'wolf' that the world has ever seen. Early European observers could not determine exactly what they were seeing: it had the head of a wolf, the stripes of a tiger, the tail of a kangaroo and the backward-opening pouch of an opossum. Its jaws were formidably strong and opened to a 180-degree angle like those of a snake. It could trot like a dog or bound over obstacles on its hind legs like a big rabbit.

To European eyes it was a strange composite animal. At various times they called it the Kangaroo Wolf, the Zebra Wolf, the Tasmanian Tiger and the Hyaena Opossum. Being a marsupial, it was, of course, unrelated to the wolf or any other member of the canine family. However, calling it a wolf was not entirely inaccurate. It was wolf-like in its general shape and habits and, within the world of marsupials, filled the evolutionary niche that the wolf did among the other mammals. One contemporary wit was not far off the mark when he called it 'a kangaroo in wolf's clothing'.

The Thylacine was the world's largest carnivorous marsupial and was the only member of both its genus and its family. Thylacines measured from 1.5 to 1.8m (5 to 6ft) in overall length, although they did not have the weight of comparably-sized members of the dog tribe. Like the true wolves, Thylacines lived in pairs or small groups, making their lairs in caves, among rock piles, or in hollow logs or trees. They spent most of their daylight hours safely hidden inside these lairs, coming out alone at dusk, night or dawn to hunt the kangaroos, wallabies and ground birds on which they fed.

Thylacines were typically marsupial, as their young (usually about four in each litter) were born in a semi-embryonic form and were then carried in their mother's shallow pouch for about three months until they were fully developed.

Like wolves, Thylacines found their prey by scent but

Thylacine   *Thylacinus cynocephalus*

tracked at a leisurely trot since they were incapable of moving at high speeds. If pressed, they would reluctantly break out into a shambling canter and, in moments of extreme emergency, would rise on to their hind legs to hop over difficult obstacles. The Thylacines' method of hunting, therefore, was not to chase flat out but to doggedly pursue their quarry until it was exhausted and unable to defend itself. Although the Pouched Wolf would not have matched the true wolf in running down its prey, it was armed with jaws and teeth that were quite incredible. Its remarkable hinged jaw that gaped to 180 degrees was far more powerful than even that of the largest Grey Wolf. And when the Thylacine finally caught its prey, it invariably killed it by instantly crushing its skull with those formidable jaws.

Despite the strength of the Thylacine, it seemed to be almost universally accepted among those with any experience of the animal that it never attacked humans unless it was trapped or at bay. When cornered by even the largest kangaroo-hunting hounds, it seemed to show little fear of them and many of these valuable dogs were killed when men used them to hunt the Thylacine.

One Tasmanian hunter named Ronald Gunn reported one such incident in which an entire pack of dogs refused to move in on an old male Thylacine once they brought it to bay. Another hunter, named H. S. Mackay, gave a graphic account of what happened when one of a pack did attack: 'A bull terrier once set upon a Wolf and bailed it up in a niche in some rocks. There the Wolf stood with its back to the wall, turning its head from side to side, checking the terrier as it tried to butt in from alternate and opposite directions. Finally the dog came in close and the Wolf gave one sharp, fox-like bite, tearing a piece of the dog's skull clean off, and it fell with the brain protruding, dead.'

Strangely enough, there are no accounts of any even moderately successful attacks on humans, even when cornered or trapped. There were odd incidents, but all seemed rather pathetic in effect and of those cases recorded all Thylacines responsible appeared to have been emaciated and almost toothless animals, either very old or near to death by starvation. These were usually easily driven away with sticks or, in one case, a child swinging a poker.

Despite its relative harmlessness to humans, the Thylacine none the less suffered the same persecution by men as the true wolf suffered throughout the world. Thylacines were given an unreasonable reputation as sheep-killers although the statistics of the day show far more sheep were killed by domestic dogs. Some settlers even revived those old European superstitions about wolves as vampires, and insisted that the Tasmanian Wolf killed only for blood. Like a vampire, they falsely claimed the Thylacine did not eat flesh, but killed only in order to suck all the blood from its victims' jugular veins. Consequently, European settlers killed every Thylacine that they could and, perhaps in reaction to this belief in its supernatural habits, frequently mutilated their corpses.

In 1888, the Tasmanian government offered a bounty for the Thylacine, although, since 1840, the Van Dieman's Land Company had set their own bounty on the animals. Between 1888 and 1914 at least 2,268 Thylacines were known to have been killed and turned in. In 1910 an epidemic rather like distemper (possibly brought in by domestic dogs) ran through the country and appears to have further reduced the already dangerously depleted population.

In 1936, the government of Tasmania totally reversed its stance and granted the Thylacine complete protection, imposing severe fines on anyone found killing the animal.

The gesture was almost absurd. The last authenticated killing of the Thylacine had been made in Mawbanna six years earlier, in 1930, and the last live specimen was captured in 1933. This one was kept in Hobart Zoo, where fortunately it was photographed and even filmed – the only such record of a live Tasmanian Thylacine in existence. This last animal died three years later. Later claims of Thylacine sightings in Tasmania were never authenticated, although two major expeditions have been launched since the 1930s to search out the animal.

Seemingly unwilling to acknowledge the extinction of this species at their own hands, in 1966 Tasmanian officials declared a huge game reserve in the south-west, extending from Low Rocky Cape to Kellista to South West Cape, where all cats, dogs and guns were prohibited. This reserve was assigned for the preservation of the Thylacine which had last been seen some thirty years before and had been exterminated by hunters who had the active support of the government.

Just when all seemed lost so far as this unique species was concerned, in 1985 astonishing new evidence came to the public notice. But strangely enough, it did not come from Tasmania. It came from Western Australia where the Thylacine (although undoubtedly a separate sub-species from the Tasmanian animal) was known only from fossil relics and was thought to have been extinct for over a thousand years. A tracker of aboriginal descent named Kevin Cameron produced photographs of what appears to be a living Thylacine. There is still considerable debate about Cameron's evidence because the photographs were hurried and are not clear enough to prove absolutely the image is that of a Thylacine.

However, if the photographs are authentic and a viable population of Thylacines is found to be living in Western Australia, this exciting turn of events may prove to be one of the most important animal discoveries of the century.

The Thylacine is just one of a long list of animals that have been hunted down with a vengeance by mankind. These animals are usually not hunted for their skins or their meat, but simply because humans have seen them as predators whose very existence constitutes a threat to human interests. Usually companies or governments have responded by imposing bounties on these animals: wolves, bears, hawks, eagles, seals, dolphins, etc.

Occasionally (and usually falsely) these animals are seen as being dangerous to human life, but more often they are seen as a threat to man's property. This 'property' may be his herds of sheep or cattle, or in many cases wild animals like deer or fish that the human often claims the other animal is 'stealing'. Whatever the case, the amount of 'damage' by the wild predator is nearly always extremely exaggerated, as is the sense of human outrage.

The wolf family appears to have been particularly singled out as a menace of the most extreme kind, when in fact its threat to human interests has been notably small. Certainly, there has been no documented case of a wild wolf ever actually tracking and killing a human. Yet throughout its wide range, the wolf has been universally vilified and hunted to the point of extermination.

In North America alone seven races of the Grey Wolf (*Canis lupus*) species and all three races of the Red Wolf (*Canis rufus*) species have been hunted to extinction this century. Besides the Thylacine, there were other wolf-like predators who shared the wolf's reputation and fate. In Chapter Five an account was given of the extinction of the Antarctic Wolf (*Dusicyon australis*) on the Falkland Islands in 1876. And in Japan there was the Shamanu or Japanese Miniature Wolf (*Canis lupus hodophilax*), a very small (84cm or 33in) animal that could not have been much of a threat, but it, too, had a bounty set on its head. The last Shamanu was hunted down and killed on Honshu in 1905.

The wolves were not the only animals to become extinct through the efforts of vengeful bounty hunters. Many predatory birds like the beautiful brown hawk called the Quelili or Guadalupe Caracara (*Polyborus lutosus*) were exterminated by bounty hunters.

After wolves, possibly the next most popular animals on the bounty hunters' list were the bears. Throughout the Northern Hemisphere, bears, like wolves, have been hunted down and, wherever possible, exterminated.

Few people realize, for instance, that there was once a native African Bear. This was the Atlas Brown Bear (*Ursus arctos crowtheri*) which was once found throughout North Africa, but during the nineteenth century had its last stronghold in the Atlas Mountains of Morocco. There, the proliferation of European guns in Morocco and Algeria brought about its final destruction. It appears to have vanished about 1870.

Another notable and regrettable bear extinction was that of the majestic Mexican Silver Grizzly (*Ursus arctos nelsoni*). The North American Brown Bear is the largest land carnivore on earth and the Mexican race was one of only four North American subspecies. The Mexican Grizzly was the very first of those great bears to come into contact with the Europeans, probably as early as 1540 when the conquistador Coronado marched from Mexico City to the Seven Cities of Cibola in New Mexico and on to the buffalo plains of Texas and Kansas.

Although it was the smallest of the four acknowledged races of the American Brown Bear, and only about half the weight and length of the Kodiak Bear, the Mexican

Grizzly was the largest native animal in all of Latin America. It measured as much as 183cm (6ft) from nose to tail and weighed anything up to 318kg (700lb), and because of its distinctive colouring, it was often called the Silver Bear or 'el oso plateado', the silver one.

By the 1930s, the Mexican Grizzly had been hunted, trapped and poisoned to such an extent that it had vanished from Arizona, New Mexico, California and Texas. In all of Mexico it could only be found in the state of Chihuahua, in the isolated mountain islands of Cerro Compano, Santa Clara and Sierro del Nido Ranges. By 1960, not more than thirty bears survived and even though a few private citizens attempted to protect this last handful of Mexican Grizzlies, others deliberately set out to destroy them. The bears were accused of raiding cattle ranches and the ranchers saw no value in allowing any of them to stay alive.

From 1961 to 1964, ranchers in the region offered rewards and engaged in an intensive campaign of poisoning, trapping and hunting this tiny surviving population. In 1964 a hunting party of ranchers went into the bear's last protected mountain retreat and found a mother bear and two cubs. Knowing full well that these may very well have been the last of the race, the ranchers brutally shot the entire family group. The Mexican Silver Grizzly was never seen again.

PART TWO

Survival

CHAPTER I

Return from Extinction

Takahe and Coelacanth

Late in the last century, that most famous of all American humorists, Mark Twain, formally addressed a large theatre audience that had come to hear the great author read from his works. However, before doing so, Twain claimed that he felt compelled to address the issue of his personal health which – a number of newspapers had reported – was not what it might be.

Indeed, the newspapers insisted the writer had actually died over a month ago! This news, claimed Mr Twain, had caused him considerable consternation. However, on discovering upon his person a few vital signs of life, he concluded these reports must be in some way incorrect.

Being a public-spirited sort of citizen, Mr Twain claimed he had delivered himself to the theatre that evening on a mission of community education. He wished to announce, to one and all, a message of some assurance. 'Reports of my death,' declared Mr Twain, 'have been somewhat exaggerated.'

In a similar vein, in the annals of natural history, there have been a number of species that for long periods of time have given every indication that they had entirely vanished from the face of the earth, only to suddenly reappear and prove that (to paraphrase Mr Twain) 'reports of their extinction have been somewhat exaggerated'.

This was certainly true in the celebrated case of the rare and beautiful Takahe (*Notornis mantelli*) of New Zealand. Notable for its distinctive red beak and striking indigo and green feathers, the Takahe was a bird so rare that only three birds of its kind had been seen in two centuries. The last of these sightings had been in 1898, yet some fifty years later in 1948 a substantial population of these 'extinct' birds was suddenly discovered on the edge of a remote mountain lake.

More recently, an elusive Indian bird called Jerdon's Doublebanded Courser (*Rhinoptilus bitorquatus*) was listed extinct after having last been seen in 1900. Numerous extensive searches were launched to find living examples, but no sign of the bird was discovered. However, in 1985, after a disappearance of eighty-five years, a local Indian hunter simply stumbled over one in the dark.

With reference to animal extinction, perhaps the remark most comparable to Mark Twain's famous announcement on his own health, was an unintentional witticism voiced by an Australian politician at the discovery of a viable population of Parma Wallabies (*Macropus parmi*).

The miniature, 30cm (1ft) tall Parma White-Fronted Wallaby is Australia's smallest kangaroo, and it was thought to have been exterminated in 1932. Its rediscovery in 1966 was greeted with some celebration.

In the wake of this discovery, a local politician made a well-meaning, but somewhat puzzling, pledge on behalf of the Australian government. 'The Parma Wallaby,' he declared, 'will never be allowed to become extinct again.'

There are a number of other examples of species that have confounded those who believed they were long gone from this world. There is one animal that must hold the all-time record for any creature being suddenly resurrected from the ranks of the extinct species of the world. Unless, by chance, someone discovers a live Brontosaurus stumbling around in a remote African swamp, most authorities in the natural sciences will not find any discovery in the twentieth century more remarkable than the one made by a sea captain off the coast of South Africa on 22 December 1938.

On that day Captain Goosens of the steam fishing trawler *EL8* pulled up its nets from a depth of 76m (250ft) and found a fish unlike any he had ever seen upon the high seas. It was a metallic blue fish with shark-like skin. It measured 1.52m (5ft) in length and weighed more than 45kg (100lb). It had a strange 'armoured' reptilian head and four curious leg-like, finny stumps on its belly, as if it were designed for walking along on the sea bottom. The big fish had a ferocious bite and proved incredibly tenacious, taking over four hours to suffocate on air after being pulled aboard the ship. Captain Goosens was convinced the fish must be at least a rarity in these waters, and soon packed the strange fish in ice. After landing in port the next day he took the specimen to South Africa's East London Museum.

The young curator of the local museum was a Miss Courtenay-Latimer, and although she was not at all a specialist in ichthyology, she knew at once the fish was something very special, and she knew she must act quickly. Although packed in ice, intense summer heat had caused the fish to begin to decay. Miss Courtenay-Latimer quickly removed the decomposing flesh and saved the skin, skeleton and head which she placed in a deep refrigeration unit. She then sent a telegram to Professor J. L. B. Smith at Albany Museum in Grahamstown, asking him to come to see the strange specimen as soon as possible.

When Professor Smith reached the East London Museum a few days later and actually examined the specimen, he was completely astonished.

It was not that the fish was unfamiliar to him. Indeed, it was a fish extremely well known to experts who studied prehistoric fossils. But that was the very point: it was an ancient fossil that had mysteriously come to life. Called a Coelacanth, it was a type of fish which had evolved some three hundred million years ago. It was from an age of fishes when no animal had yet climbed out of the water to live on dry land.

During the following two hundred million years, the Coelacanth did not change at all, but this was the time when amphibians and reptiles began to invade all the land masses until at last they evolved into the great Dinosaurs, who for so long ruled as the dominant life form on the planet. It was during the last few million years of the Age of the Dinosaurs that all known scientific evidence suggested the last of the Coelacanths became extinct.

Under the circumstances, one may forgive Professor Smith's sense of wonder. It seemed impossible that here was a Coelacanth, some seventy million years after it was thought to have become extinct. Yet here it was, large as life, and when first caught quite willing to try to bite off a fisherman's hand in order to prove it. The naturalist-author Herbert Wendt rather accurately described the professor's reaction: 'As Professor Smith looked at the fish, he felt as though Miss Courtenay-Latimer had shown him a newly killed dinosaur.'

In any case, Professor Smith wasted no time in announcing this remarkable discovery to the world. In honour of the curator and the place it was found, Professor Smith named this Coelacanth the *Latimeria chalumnae*. It was soon being called the most important single

Coelacanth   *Latimeria chalumnae*

zoological discovery of the century, and the 'fish that time forgot'.

With its amphibian-like skull and four strange leg-like fins, it was considered by some to be a kind of fish-amphibian 'missing-link'. As a living example of a 'fin-footed fish' – or, as some liked to call it, 'the fish with four legs' – it was a creature that, against all odds, had remained unchanged for hundreds of millions of years.

Coelacanths are important because they represent a structural stage in the evolution of fishes corresponding to the point when the first steps on land were taken. This 'living fossil' is a representative of that age when the first fin-footed fish raised itself up from the primeval waters on its stumpy little 'legs' and 'walked' on land. This was a momentous event in evolutionary history which first led to the development of amphibians, then reptiles and eventually birds and mammals.

Anxious to find more examples of this extraordinary creature, Professor Smith offered what at the time was a substantial reward of £100 for anyone who would supply him with another specimen. He advertised and sent leaflets with diagrams and descriptions of the Coelacanth throughout Southern Africa, but no replies were forthcoming.

It was not until some fourteen years after that first discovery that an Englishman named Captain Hunt decided that he had heard rumours of such a fish among the Comoro Islanders. Hunt had read of Professor Smith's quest for the Coelacanth and enlisted the help of local Comoro fishermen, issuing them all drawings of the fish.

Soon after, in December 1952, a fisherman named Ahmed Hussein was passing through a local fish market on the island of Anjouan in the Comoros. And there, sitting in a stall, was a little man with the fabled Coelacanth. It was to be sold to whomever wanted to make fish steaks out of it. It was 1.52m (5ft) long, and it weighed almost as much as the fisherman did, but he claimed he had simply caught the fish from a rocky shore on the island with a hook and line.

Ahmed Hussein seized the fish and took the merchant back to see Captain Hunt. Hunt recognized the fish and purchased it. He then immediately injected the fish with preservative and put it on ice. Next, he telegraphed Professor Smith in Grahamstown. The excited professor flew to Anjouan on 29 December to confirm Hunt's finding, and the world had its second example of this remarkable fish.

In the following years, it was proved that the first Coelacanth caught off the coast of South Africa was a stray which had been swept by ocean currents far to the south of its home waters. Its real habitat is the waters around the Comoro Islands in the Indian Ocean. These islands lie in the northernmost part of the Mozambique Channel, between Mozambique and Madagascar, and are French controlled. The French authorities took up the hunt and, between 1953 and 1955, another six Coelacanths had been discovered. Since then a considerable number of these fish have been caught, and today most major national museums of the world have acquired at least one specimen.

It now seems that the Comoro Islanders had known the fish for some time without, of course, being aware of its unique status. It was evidently not uncommon to sell it in the fish markets like the one Ahmed Hussein had visited. And like that one, they were usually caught with fishing lines and baited hooks in relatively shallow waters near the island shores. The French researchers were in fact told that for many decades before its 'discovery' by the outside world, the Comoro Islanders had often used the

Coelacanth's rough skin as a substitute for sandpaper when repairing bicycle-tyre punctures. A rather novel use for the famous 'living fossil'!

Today, the Coelacanth does not have a large population, but it appears to be stable. There is still considerable discussion about its position on the evolutionary ladder, but it remains a creature of enormous interest to evolutionary biologists: the long lost 'lobe-finned fish' that staggered into the twentieth century like some sort of underwater dinosaur some seventy million years after its believed extinction.

CHAPTER 2

Eleventh Hour Revivals

Golden Hamster and
Przewalski's Wild Horse

T he year 1930 saw the start of the most spectacular recovery from almost certain extinction in zoological history. It is a story that begins like a detective novel.

The bookish detective of this tale was a Palestinian scholar named Professor Aharoni who first stumbled across clues to a kind of zoological mystery in some ancient and obscure scrolls. From his reading of ancient Aramaic texts, Professor Aharoni gradually became aware of a strange little animal unknown to science in modern times. His curiosity aroused, the professor searched out all references to the creature. It appeared to be a domestic pet particularly popular with Assyrian children in ancient times. From the texts he understood it to be 'a special kind of Syrian mouse, which was brought to Assyria and into the land of the Hittites', but from its descriptions it was certainly unlike any mouse now known, and no one in the twentieth century was known to keep such animals as pets anywhere in the regions described.

Undeterred by the fact that there had been no records of these elusive animals for over a thousand years, the professor set himself the task of finding some physical evidence of the creature. If he was lucky, he thought, he might find a skeleton or a skull.

The texts the professor had read all referred to the 'mouse' being most common in the ancient Hittite city of Chaleb. However, Chaleb had been destroyed in ancient times and was nothing but a ruin, although the modern city of Aleppo had grown up on the site. Professor Aharoni set off for Aleppo and spent his days diligently searching for traces of what he expected to be the extinct Syrian Mouse. Instead, he discovered a tiny burrow with an entire family of thirteen furry, red-gold rodents.

What Professor Aharoni had found, against unimaginable odds, was the very last population of the ancient Assyrian and Hittite house pet that had struggled for survival in the wild over the past millennium. Remarkably, no one in modern times had ever recorded sighting these animals before, and even more remarkably – despite exhaustive searches since – no one was ever to find them in the wild after that single discovery by the intrepid Professor Aharoni.

Even more astonishing was the rate of recovery of this wild population of thirteen rodents, for these animals proved to be what is now the common and extremely popular household pet called the Golden Hamster (*Mesocricetus auratus*)! Taken into protective captivity, the tiny population suddenly multiplied in the most astounding manner. Aharoni could not give the offspring away fast enough. Indeed, the Golden Hamster is capable of producing young after a pregnancy of just fifteen to sixteen days. This is the shortest gestation period of any mammal with fully developed young. Within a decade, the world population of Golden Hamsters rose from thirteen to several million.

No one now would list the Golden Hamster as a rare species. Today there are hundreds of breeds and strains of Hamsters and their world population has grown to a hundred million and more. It seems almost impossible to believe this massive population could be descended from those original thirteen animals discovered by Professor Aharoni in 1930, but this is certainly the case. Without doubt, the Golden Hamster holds the record for the fastest recovery from endangered status in the annals of zoological science.

Although the Golden Hamster's history is unique, it is not the only species to be reduced to what would appear to be almost impossibly small numbers, then to turn around and make a sudden and substantial recovery. There have been a considerable number of these last-minute rescue operations where dedicated individuals have taken a seemingly doomed wild population and successfully bred them in captivity, thus saving the species from extinction.

Golden Hamster   *Mesocricetus auratus*

One remarkable case was that of Przewalski's Wild Horse (*Equus przewalskii*), the only undomesticated horse species to survive into the twentieth century. It is a short, stocky horse with a gold-brown or gold-red coat, a black mohawk-style mane and a long black tail. It was discovered by the Russian scholar, Nikolai Przewalski, in the Gobi desert in 1879.

At the time of its discovery there was one other true Wild Horse which lived in the steppe land of southern Russia – the Tarpan (*Equus ferus*). These animals were the horses known to Ice Age man and are the two true ancestors of all domestic horses. However, the grey-coated, rugged little Tarpan was so ruthlessly hunted that by 1887 it was extinct, leaving Przewalski's Wild Horse the only surviving Wild Horse left in the world.

The Przewalski's Wild Horse appears to be now extinct in the wild, although there are persistent rumours of occasional sightings of individuals or pairs of animals from time to time in the region of the Gobi desert. Initially, because of Przewalski's discovery and the acquisition of some fifty animals between 1897 and 1902 by western zoos and collectors, captive-bred animals did survive. But by 1956 even these animals – not having the reproductive powers of the hamster – had dwindled to just thirty-six individuals. As these last animals were scattered all over the world in various zoos and collections, there was no single breeding pool to regenerate the species. It was obvious that unless urgent and co-ordinated action was taken the species would soon become extinct in captivity as well as in the wild.

By the end of the 1950s, a strong interest in this unique species had developed. A number of captive breeding programmes were established; most notably in Prague, Czechoslovakia, and in the Catskills in America. A proper Przewalski's Wild Horse stud book registration system was established, and by 1976 there were 250 registered animals.

Today there are more than 500 of these Ice Age Wild Horses. Thanks to the efforts of the Wild Horse enthusiasts, the species now seems out of danger so far as the extinction of its captive population is concerned. Furthermore, there are now plans afoot to attempt to restore some of these animals to their wild state in their ancient Mongolian homeland, where it is hoped they may form the basis of a new free-roaming population.

CHAPTER 3

Public Campaign and Political Lobby

Great Whales

The whales are the Grand Canyons and the Mount Everests of the animal world. The heart of the Blue Whale is the height of a tall man and weighs half a ton. It beats like a huge kettle drum and its valves pump a sea of hot blood along the whale's 30.5m (100ft), 160-ton bulk, through arteries so big a child could crawl through them.

Whales have been the largest-brained creatures on this planet for thirty times longer than the human race. The largest brain ever evolved is that of the Sperm Whale which, at up to 10kg (22lb), is more than six times the size of the human brain. The Bowhead Whale has a mouth as wide as a car ferry which would allow two semi-trailer trucks to enter side by side. The Humpback Whale sings songs that can be heard over miles of open ocean. The Killer Whale propels itself beyond the explanations of science at speeds of 64km (40 miles) per hour and is the fastest animal in the sea.

The whales are the emblematic animals for conservationists worldwide. If these amazing animals, the largest ever to exist on the planet, cannot be saved from the ruthless exploitation of a handful of men, what chance of survival have any other species? Around the conservaists' banners to Save the Whales, scientists, teachers, actors, comedians, singers, schoolchildren, doctors, lawyers and even a few Indian chiefs have gathered. Supporters have come from every profession, political persuasion, age, group and race.

Against them stand the men who hunt the whale. They are few, but they are men of influence, who are determined to continue and refuse, in the face of all evidence, to see or believe the consequences of their actions. Such men in other times have brought about the extinction of the Passenger Pigeon, the Greak Auk, the Steller's Sea Cow, the Blue Buck, the Caribbean Monk Seal, the Bali Tiger and a hundred others. Such men push species after species into the oblivion of extinction and call it honest industry; a work ethic that would stop the heart of all life on the planet if some means might be found to profit by it.

The public campaigns and political lobbies established to save the whales have been the largest and most sophisticated of any in the conservation movement. And some of the developments have been the most remarkable and highly visible in the history of the conservation movement.

It was really the environmental activists of Greenpeace who first brought the public campaign to save the whales into front-page news. It was Greenpeace's direct action tactics in 1975 when they took their inflatable speedboats and tried to stand between the whales and the Soviet whaling fleet – the massive ten-storey high, 230m (750ft) Soviet factory ship, the *Vostok*, and her fleet of six harpoon boats – that gave the movement its first real international television coverage and brought the struggle to the world's attention.

And it was such tactics that kept the public campaign going. The inflatable zodiacs became the standard ecological floating pickets used to block whalers' harpoons. There were many variations: blockades, ship-boardings and even activists who chained themselves to the harpoon guns. Over the next few years, Greenpeace and others took dozens of direct protest actions against the Russians, Japanese, Australians, Icelanders and Spaniards. Harpoons were fired over their heads, protesters were arrested, ships were seized and held, but still the activists persisted.

These flamboyant actions, combined with more traditional methods, such as public rallies, petitions, publicity campaigns and political lobbying, were quite successful, but the whaling industry responded by creating fleets of pirate factory ships which hunted illegally and totally without control.

These pirate whaling ships, which were secretly owned by the Japanese, refused to recognize any quotas, closed seasons, protected territorial waters or protected species and even ignored bans on hunting nursing mothers and suckling young. The extreme illegality of these ships and the reluctance of any government to do anything about them resulted in some of the most radical actions of the entire conservation movement.

In 1979, the conservationist ship, *Sea Shepherd*, rammed and crippled the illegal pirate whaler, the *Sierra*, just outside the port of Leixoes, Portugal. Seven months later in February 1980, anonymous anti-whaling activists used bombs to sink the same pirate whaling ship in Lisbon harbour, Portugal. Nearly three months later, the two Spanish whalers, *Ibsa I* and *Ibsa II*, were also sunk by the same team of anonymous activists.

Although no one had been hurt in the sinking of the whaling ships, Greenpeace and nearly all other conservationist groups stated that they totally disapproved of such dangerous tactics in this cause. They argued that they might indeed be willing to endanger their own lives to save the whales, but they were not willing to endanger anyone else.

Meanwhile, other activists succeeded through environmental espionage in working behind the scenes to have other pirate whaling ventures closed. In South Africa two pirate whaling ships were seized and destroyed. In the Philippines and in Taiwan no less than five pirate whaling ships were put out of business through environmental investigations which led to political lobbying and government actions against the whalers.

Since the extreme actions of 1979–80, there have been a number of other direct action offensives, such as the *Sea Shepherd* and Greenpeace invasions of the Siberian whaling grounds in 1981 and 1982, and the devastating 1987 attack by *Sea Shepherd* agents in Iceland, in which the eco-saboteurs successfully scuttled two Icelandic whaling ships and demolished the country's only whaling station.

However, despite the dramatic nature of the gladiatorials between ecologists and whalers on the high seas that have kept the public campaign to save the whales alive, many of the most vital battles in the whale war have been and still are being waged around conference negotiating tables, in government legislatures, and in court rooms.

High points for the political lobbyists and the diplomats of the movement were: the unanimous United Nations call for a ban on commercial whaling that in 1972 gave a platform for the whole movement; the 1979 US Senate Packwood–Magnusson Amendment, which threatened sanctions against violators of whaling regulations; and, most astonishing of all, the winning in 1982 of a two-thirds majority vote in the whalers' own organization, the International Whaling Commission, to declare a moratorium on commercial whaling. This last victory in the IWC should have legally ended all commercial whaling by

1985; Japan, Norway, and Iceland have, however, refused to abide by this and every other ruling which has
ordered an end to whaling – and so the battle goes on.

The Save the Whales movement has achieved some
astonishing successes, and it has certainly saved several
whale populations from extinction. It is probably the best
example of how the combination of public campaigning
and political lobbying has been able to change public
opinion and government policy in the cause of conservation. Through such tactics, the Indian Ocean has been
declared a whale sanctuary. Since activists began their
actions, whaling has ceased in Australia, South Africa,
Taiwan, Korea, Spain, Portugal and Brazil, among
others. Indeed, commercial whaling has ceased in the
national waters of all but three countries. Pirate operations
in a score of countries have been forced to close down
operations. Perhaps most remarkably of all, one of the last
two giant whaling nations, the Soviet Union, retired its
factory fleet in 1987.

Yet it seems likely that Japan, Norway and Iceland will
still hunt the whale right into the 1990s. Considering the
breadth and depth of world-wide support for the movement, it is the tenacity of the whalers that is remarkable.
By 1982, the conflict had reached such a level that all
treaty and legal agreements that govern or relate to the
whaling industry ruled that after 1985 all commercial
whaling operations must stop. Since 1985, with the exception of aboriginal hunting, all whalers are considered
pirate operators. And yet it goes on. Why?

There is only one reason. A very few people are making
large profits in virtually the only market for the product
remaining in the world: Japan. All commercial whaling
(and certainly all pirate whaling) has continued for the
past twenty years simply to supply the Japanese market
with whale meat. This market, which buys and sells legal

or smuggled meat indiscriminately, is a totally unneces-
sary and quite frivolous food-fad market in a wealthy and
powerful nation which could stop it without any incon-
venience to anyone. In the last analysis, the whaling
industry continues to slaughter whales only because of the
pressure a few wealthy fishing industrialists can bring to
bear on a handful of corrupt politicians in the Japanese
government.

Without doubt, the Grey Whale (*Eschrichtius robustus*) is
one of twelve Great Whale species that would certainly
have become extinct had it not been for the extensive
public campaigns and political lobbies which resulted in
laws being passed to protect it and other marine mammals.
   The Grey Whale is quite different from all other whale
species; its most obvious physical characteristic is its
mottled, grey coloration and its patchy, often barnacled
skin. It grows to a maximum of 15m (50ft) and a weight of
thirty-five tons or more.
   Originally, there were three races or geographic populations of Grey Whale, all of which migrated along the
coasts of the great continents on their long migration
routes. There was the Atlantic Grey Whale which European coastal whale hunters seem to have exterminated by
the eighteenth century. There was also the Western
Pacific Grey Whale of the Asian coast that the Japanese
and Russian whalers had eliminated by 1933. Today, only
the Eastern Pacific race of Grey Whale survives. This race
migrates along the west coast of North America.
   The migration of the Grey Whale – the longest annual
migration of any mammal – is astounding. It makes a
yearly voyage of about 16,000km (10,000 miles) from the
Arctic Sea to the lagoons of the Baja peninsula in Mexico.
   Grey Whales feed for four months, from June to
September, in the shallow Arctic waters of the Chukchi

Grey Whale   *Eschrichtius robustus*

and Bering Seas. (They are the only bottom-feeding Whales, diving down to feed on tiny 2.5cm (1in.) long crustaceans that live on the sandy sea beds of the Arctic seas.) In October through to December, the Grey Whales migrate southward to Mexico. During January and February they breed and mate (usually in alternate years), then they return northward from March through May to the high Arctic. During migration, the Whales swim continuously for three months each way. They cover over 106km (66 miles) a day, and for the entire eight months of migration and breeding, Grey Whales go virtually without food or sleep.

The survival of the last race of this remarkable animal on the west coast of North America was not at all certain. Indeed, the whaling industry was believed to have exterminated the species – not once, but twice – in the last hundred years.

Discovery in 1855 of the breeding grounds of the Grey Whale in the hidden lagoons of the Baja Peninsula in Mexico resulted in an unprecedented massacre. Being a coast-hugging species in its migration pattern, the Grey Whales always were a vulnerable species, and once the breeding grounds were found, there appeared to be no escape from extermination. Once the whalers entered the closed lagoons, the whales could not escape in the shallow water. They had no shelter either to mate or give birth, and all were killed without discrimination. From 1855 to 1865, ten thousand out of a total population of fifteen thousand Grey Whales were wiped out. By 1890, the rest of the population was killed, and whalers could not find any Grey Whales along their migration routes or in any known breeding lagoon on the Baja coast.

It appears, however, that somehow a small Grey Whale population went into hiding. They must have found other shallow lagoons along the uninhabited Mexican coast to breed in. During the First World War years a few Grey Whales were spotted and once again Norwegian, Japanese and Soviet whalers went out and found an exploitable Grey Whale population. Learning nothing from the species' near-extinction in the previous century, they continued to hunt whales until they vanished once again just before the Second World War.

In 1946, the International Whaling Commission finally gave the Grey Whale full protected status, but as many pointed out, the organization only did so because the species now appeared to be so close to extinction that whalers no longer found it worthwhile to look for it. It was this protected status, plus a number of other protective measures and national conservationist laws gained through public awareness campaigns and political lobbying groups, that in the long run saved the Grey Whale.

Strangely enough, the Grey Whale's coast-hugging migration route and its limited breeding- and feeding-ground habitats which originally made this animal so vulnerable, eventually allowed for its salvation. For once the United States, Canada and Mexico defined protected coastal reserves for the animal the species could be protected, as its entire coastal migration route was within their territorial waters.

With most other whale species, this has not been possible. Although the Blue Whales and the Right Whales have been supposedly protected far longer than the Grey Whale, they have never recovered from the devastations of the whaling industry. The Blue Whale, after over fifty years of protection, is believed to have survived in numbers equivalent to only 2 per cent of its original population. The Right Whale, after over sixty years of protection, is at less than 1 per cent of its original population.

The Grey Whale is, in fact, the only whale species to have actually recovered from the destruction wrought on it by the whaling industry and is the one Great Whale species that can truly be said to have been 'saved' by the conservation movement. It is now believed to have reached over 15,000 animals, which is its full original population.

Today, the Grey Whale migrations and their spectacular leaping mating rituals make these animals one of the wonders of the natural world. Hundreds of thousands of people come each year to watch the Grey Whales migrate past Cabrillo National Monument at Point Lomo, San Diego. Perhaps a million others watch from look-out points elsewhere along the Mexican, American and Canadian coast lines each year. And film makers come in droves to make nature films of these titanic animals hurling themselves about in the shallow, but now safe, waters of their traditional mating lagoons.

CHAPTER 4

National Totems

Mountain Gorilla
and Giant Panda

Since prehistoric times, people have seen certain characteristics in animals which they admire, and they have adopted these as emblematic animals for their tribe, race or nation. This is no less true today than it was in ancient times. Most nations have at least one animal that serves as a kind of national totem. Sometimes they are exotic or even mythical animals: lion for Britain, unicorn for France. However, most often they are animals native to those countries: bear for Russia, eagle for the United States, elephant for India, beaver for Canada, kangaroo for Australia, kiwi for New Zealand.

Like most tribal people who adopt a totem animal, most nations take an active concern in survival of these special animals and, in modern times, have often found it necessary to take measures to guard against the possibility of those animals becoming extinct.

In the twentieth century, there have been a number of creatures that have been saved from over-exploitation by becoming national totems. The eagle in America and the beaver in Canada were both species that were becoming endangered because of overhunting until appeals to national pride successfully mobilized the governments of these nations and the totemic animals were protected and revived.

Realizing how successful such tactics can be, conservationists have often lobbied for the adoption of some unique national or state animal in an attempt to save a species from extinction. This is certainly true of most American states. A few years ago conservationists convinced Connecticut to adopt the Sperm Whale as its state animal. Consequently, Connecticut has taken an active interest in the Save the Whale movement world-wide. The spectacularly beautiful and nearly extinct Monkey-eating Eagle had a new lease of life when it was renamed the Philippine Eagle and became the national bird. Laws were immediately passed for its protection and it was granted a territorial refuge and a captive breeding programme was funded by the federal government.

Similarly, it was largely because of the celebrity status achieved by the Mountain Gorillas through the work of the dedicated conservationist Dian Fossey that the African nation of Rwanda acquired these remarkable animals as national totems. Although Mountain Gorillas are among the world's most endangered species, the three hundred or so remaining animals may very well survive because of their special status in this small, poor African nation. Rwanda will ensure their continued existence for a long time to come as the animals will continue to be a major source of income through tourism.

One of the best known and certainly most popular of all the more recently acquired national totems must be the Giant Panda (*Ailuropoda melanoleuca*) of China. Rare, exotic, cuddly, playful, gentle and strikingly handsome, the Giant Panda – ever since the world beyond China learned of its existence – has been one of the most popular animals on the planet. It was not until quite recently, however, that China itself learned of the Panda's great powers as an international diplomat and ambassador of goodwill for the Chinese nation. Today it is a national treasure. Although it is a very rare animal – probably no more than 1,000 exist – the Chinese have recently taken the species' survival very much to heart, banning all hunting absolutely, and only allowing capture with government approval on a national level.

The Panda has always been a rare and mysterious beast. There are a few ancient Chinese written accounts of the trade in skins of these animals – usually called 'Bei-shung' or 'white bear' – in ancient Chinese writings. Even in ancient times the Panda was extremely rare and made its home largely in the remote bamboo forests of mountainous Szechwan province, so the Chinese themselves were largely unaware of this secretive animal's existence.

The story of the coming of the first Pandas to the West is a dramatic and surprisingly recent one. Western science was first to learn of the existence of this mysterious animal through the explorations of a remarkable French priest, Father Armand David. Father David, or Père David as he is usually known, was a Jesuit priest who became the greatest authority of his time on Chinese flora and fauna. In 1869 Père David first heard of this mysterious animal and was shown a skin by a hunter in the remote mountainous and forested regions of the southern province of Szechwan. In the following weeks, Père David was able to acquire two skins of his own by paying local hunters to track the animals down. He made notes on how the animal was totally unlike any other species of bear in many structural aspects, and also as it lived almost entirely on bamboo. Soon after, when Père David's Chinese bear skins arrived in Paris and were called various names from Harlequin Bear to Bamboo Bear, it was immediately established that they belonged to a unique species.

And unique the Giant Panda certainly is; even today there is considerable debate about how to classify the animal. Some classify it as an early form of bear, others as a specialized member of the racoon family, others still believe it should be classified in a family grouping uniquely its own. Today, everyone is familiar with the general appearance of the Giant Panda and generally think

Giant Panda   *Ailuropoda melanoleuca*

of it as a large, living cuddly toy. A large adult Giant Panda, however, grows up to weigh as much as 135kg (300lb) and measures up to 1.8m (6ft) in length. When born the animal is entirely white and weighs less than 450g (1lb), but grows to about 30kg (70lb) within a year. It is quite a solitary animal, living alone in areas of bamboo and coniferous forest and foraging for vast quantities of bamboo shoots every day. The Giant Panda makes itself beds of bamboo in lairs under the shelter of hollow trees or overhanging rocks and lives at altitudes of between 2,500 and 4,000m (8,000 and 13,000ft) in a generally cold and humid climate. Unlike other bears, in the extreme cold of winter, the Panda does not hibernate but simply moves further down the mountainside out of the worst of the weather. The life span of the Giant Panda is believed to be a little over fifteen years.

After Père David's initial discovery of the Giant Panda, six more skins reached the West through traders over the next several decades but very little further information came out of China about this mysterious animal. In fact, it was nearly another fifty years before a westerner actually saw a live Giant Panda.

This happened in the year 1916, when the German zoologist Hugo Weigold went on an expedition into West China and Tibet and, through local hunters, actually acquired a live infant Panda. Sadly the infant did not survive long and died shortly after Weigold bought it. Still, this would normally have been a remarkable encounter, at least in scientific circles, but as this expedition had been launched by Germans in the midst of World War I, Weigold's news did not reach Britain or America. Even a decade or more afterwards, other adventurers who set out in search of the Giant Panda were unaware of Weigold's first encounter with a living Panda.

Up to now, all the Giant Pandas had been killed or

captured by Chinese hunters or the Lolo tribesmen who inhabited the region and no westerner could claim to have personally tracked down and shot a Giant Panda. As might be expected, this sort of challenge appealed less to the zoologists and more to the big-game hunting fraternity.

In 1928, two hunters achieved their greatest ambition. At enormous cost, the Americans Theodore and Kermit Roosevelt set out on a highly publicized expedition to track down the Giant Panda. It seems somewhat ironic that these two intrepid hunters were the sons of the American President Theodore (or Teddy) Roosevelt. After all, the famous 'Teddy Bear' was named after Roosevelt by a toy manufacturer when the press reported how the President proved too soft-hearted to shoot a little brown bear cub while on a hunting trip, and insisted on it being released. Kermit and Theodore Jr had no such pangs of conscience when tracking down the Giant Panda – the future challenger to the Teddy Bear as the child's favourite cuddly toy. Determined to become the first great white hunters to bag a Giant Panda, their hearts did not soften when the opportunity came.

Kermit Roosevelt wrote of that first fatal encounter with the Panda in his book *Trailing the Giant Panda*:

'On the morning of the 13th of April we came upon Giant Panda tracks in the snow near Yehli, south of Tachienlu in the Hsifan Mountains. The animal had evidently passed a goodish while before the snow ceased falling, but some sign that one of the Lolos found proved to be recent enough to thoroughly arouse all four natives . . .

'We had been following the trail for two and a half hours when we came to a more open jungle. Unexpectedly close I heard a clicking chirp. One of the Lolo hunters darted forward. He had not gone forty yards before he turned back to eagerly motion to us to hurry. As I gained his side he pointed to a giant spruce thirty yards away. The bole was hollowed, and from it emerged the head and forequarters of a Beishung. He looked sleepily from side to side as he sauntered forth and walked slowly away into the bamboos. As soon as Ted came up we fired simultaneously at the outline of the disappearing Panda. Both shots took effect. He was a splendid old male, the first that the Lolos had any record of as being killed in this Yehli region. Our great good fortune could only with much effort be credited. After so long holding aloof, the Hunting Gods had turned about and brewed the unusual chain of circumstances that alone could enable us to shoot a Giant Panda, trailing him without dogs and with the crowning bit of luck that permitted us to fire jointly.'

It is hard for most people today to feel much joy in this account of the killing of this gentle, harmless animal, but it was a major event at the time, and most of the main natural history institutes in the world wanted their own Giant Panda skins. For the next decade, despite their acknowledged rarity and the very real possibility of their near-extinct status, there was an all-out attempt to track down and kill as many Giant Pandas as possible. A number of expeditions were sent out to hunt them down and discover as much as could be found out about them. One expedition leader went so far as to test out the Panda as a source of food (the local people did not eat the animals) and was the first – and hopefully the last – westerner to eat Giant Panda steaks. Fortunately for the animal the steaks proved very tough, and it was thought that even as Panda hamburger, it would not be very palatable.

By 1936, a total of nearly thirty Giant Pandas had been slaughtered for western collections. By that time, it occurred to some westerners that as rare and exciting as the acquisition of Giant Pandas for the purpose of stuffing and displaying might be, the acquisition of a live specimen as a zoo animal would have enormous public appeal.

And so, once again, another great Giant Panda race was on. Who would be the first to bring in a live Giant Panda?

Considering the difficulty of even finding live animals to shoot, many thought the elusive animal would prove next to impossible to trap alive. However, in 1936, there were two front-runners in this race: an experienced animal collector with the colourful and unlikely name of Floyd Tangier Smith and a New York fashion designer named Ruth Harkness. Floyd Tangier Smith had spent over a decade in the region and had helped acquire a number of Panda skins for collectors. Ruth Harkness had never been to the Orient before and knew next to nothing about Giant Pandas, except that it had been her late husband's dream to capture one.

Tangier Smith and most others with knowledge of the bandit-ridden region thought it preposterous that a woman should even attempt to travel in Panda territory, let alone embark on such an impossible mission as actually to capture one. But Ruth Harkness penetrated the extraordinary wilderness with terrific tenacity, and captured a baby Giant Panda with the help of the Chinese-American hunter Quentin Young.

In her book *The Lady and the Panda*, Ruth Harkness writes with some humour about the almost unbelievably difficult time she had in making it into Panda country. On the critical day in November when they neared their quarry at last, Ruth Harkness describes her far from dignified pursuit. With Quentin Young and a local hunter ahead of her, she was making her way through the undergrowth:

'. . . mostly on hands and knees, only Yang remained behind to give me an occasional lift by the seat of my

pants. Without warning, a shout went up from the jungle
ahead of us. I heard Lao yell, the report of his blunderbuss
musket, and then Quentin's voice raised in rapid and
imperious Chinese. Falling, stumbling, or being dragged
by Yang, we crashed through the bamboo.'

A full-grown Giant Panda had crossed their trail and
one of the hunters, against instruction, had fired his gun.
The frightened animal fled, but Quentin Young and Ruth
Harkness did not follow the hunters.

'We listened for a moment, and went on a few yards
farther where the bamboo thinned slightly, giving way to a
few big trees. Quentin stopped so short that I almost fell
over him. He listened intently for a split second, and then
went ploughing on so rapidly I couldn't keep up with him.
Dimly through the waving wet branches I saw him near a
huge rotting tree. I too stopped, frozen in my tracks.
From the old dead tree came a baby's whimper. I must
have been momentarily paralyzed, for I didn't move until
Quentin came toward me and held out his arms. There in
the palms of his two hands was a squirming baby
Beishung.'

It was a ten-day-old Panda weighing less than three
pounds. Its eyes were still closed and Ruth Harkness
bottle-fed the animal and raised it like a kitten. She named
it Su-Lin which means 'something very cute'. After
numerous other adventures attempting to get her little
passenger safely out of China, Ruth Harkness at last
succeeded in bringing the first live Giant Panda to the
West.

So the first Giant Panda to reach the West alive found
its home in the Brookfield Zoo in Chicago in 1937, and the
following year was joined by a second Giant Panda called
Mei-Mei, which again was captured by Ruth Harkness.

Meanwhile, the intrepid Floyd Tangier Smith proved
he was not entirely out of the Giant Panda competitions.

In 1938, Tangier Smith arrived in England on a ship packed with no less than five live Pandas, tentatively called Grandma, Happy, Dopey, Grumpy and Baby. The last three were purchased by the London Zoo and renamed Sung, Tang and Ming.

Only six more live Giant Pandas were to be exported to the West before the Chinese government in 1941 placed an absolute ban on their export. With only one exception, there were no more live Pandas allowed outside China for sixteen years. In some respects this was something of a blessing, for zoos knew too little of these animals to care for them properly. Of the fourteen animals reaching the West only four survived more than four years, and only one more than ten years, and so for a time there were no Giant Pandas at all in zoos.

However, between 1957 and 1959, a total of three Giant Pandas were presented by the Chinese government. Two of these (called Ping-Ping and An-An) went to the Moscow Zoo, and one (called Chi-Chi) to the London Zoo. Fortunately, understanding of Panda habits and biology had increased to some degree and these zoos proved safer places for the animals than before. Although Ping-Ping died in 1961, Chi-Chi and An-An went on to break all records and were both nearly fifteen years old when they died. For all of that time these animals were the only live Pandas in existence outside China.

In 1972, all that was to change, for the Chinese government opened its doors to the West. As a historic gesture, when Richard Nixon became the first American President to visit China, the Chinese government made a gift of a Giant Panda to the Washington Zoo. The West once again had a Giant Panda.

Since then, about twenty Giant Pandas have been officially presented to national governments as tokens of friendship, and an international effort launched by such organizations as the World Wildlife Fund has been made to protect the species in the wild. The Chinese government has matched the enthusiasm of these organizations and set up over a hundred reserves and a number of study centres. The animals are notoriously difficult to breed in captivity, although institutions in China have had noted successes, and artificial insemination programmes look likely to be established in the future.

Today more is known about Giant Pandas than ever before, but essentially they remain rare, mysterious and fascinating creatures. Now that the Chinese government and the international conservation community have taken an active and protective interest in the animal, its survival seems likely. It appears as if the thousand or so Giant Pandas left may very well have established a secure place on this planet – and they will have succeeded in doing so largely by establishing a secure place in the hearts of members of the human race.

CHAPTER 5

Royal Patronage

Hangul and
Père David's Deer

For the greater part of human history, it has been a royal prerogative and passion to collect exotic and beautiful animals in private menageries and game reserves. Indeed, the collection and display of strange and unusual birds and beasts since ancient times have become as much a part of royal and aristocratic status as grand palaces and ostentatious wealth.

The attitudes and degree of enlightenment of these early animal collectors varied considerably. The majority of animals were protected simply to give aristocrats a ready supply of victims for sports hunting. Many accounts of royal hunts in India, Africa, Asia and Europe describe the carnage when thousands of animals (many of them endangered species) were slaughtered. The detailed descriptions of such hunts often leave contemporary readers astonished at the obvious frivolity and waste of such 'sport'.

Still, it must be recognized that among the many royal and aristocratic families, there have been some enlightened and inspired enthusiasts without whom the survival of many animal species would not have been possible. Certainly, until the mid-nineteenth century when popular sympathies began to be aroused with a view to preserving

vanishing species, it was largely the enthusiasm of aristocratic natural historians and royal patrons that allowed a
number of species to survive.

It is true, for instance, that the Wisent or European
Bison (*Bison bonasus*) would not have survived the last
three centuries had not the Russian czars protected them
and eventually established two huge imperial preserves in
the Bialowieska Forest in Poland and the mountainous
Caucasian region of south-west Russia. Similarly, the rare
and magnificent Kashmir Stag or Hangul (*Cervus elaphus
hanglu*) survived in the Dachigam Forests only because it
was considered the royal stag and the property of the
Maharajah of Kashmir. Also, the last two hundred wild
Asiatic Lions (*Panthera leo persica*) in the world owe their
continued existence to the fact that the Nawab of Juna-
gardh gave the beasts sanctuary in his 1,300km (500 sq.
miles) Gir Forest preserve in India.

Even today we find that the role of royalty in the
preservation of species is considerable. Two of the most
prominent figures and guiding lights of the World Wildlife
Fund have been Prince Philip and Prince Bernhardt of the
Netherlands. Their involvement in large-scale conservation programmes has helped to draw many other sym-
pathetic members of royal and aristocratic families to the
cause. This has been as true in India and the Arab states as
it has been among the European nations which still have
prominent royal families.

Perhaps the most remarkable and unlikely case of royal
patronage proving to be the salvation of a species is a
story which involves the unlikely alliance of the Chinese
emperors, an English duke, and a French priest.

The priest was Father Armand David, or Père David,
and now famous as the first European to discover the
Giant Panda. Armand David's father was a physician who

gave his son a sound education in zoology and botany before the boy eventually went into the priesthood. In 1861, at the age of twenty-five, the young priest was sent off to China to work as a missionary. During his eleven-year stay in the Orient, besides his missionary work, he became the most noted European expert on Chinese natural history. Beyond his discovery of both the Giant and Lesser Pandas, his discoveries of plants, insects, birds and mammals unknown to European science were legion. Along with the discovery of the pandas, Père David is best known for the discovery of a rare and very unusual species of deer.

The Chinese called the animal 'Ssepu Hsiang', which evidently translates as 'not deer, not ox, not goat, not donkey'. The reason for this peculiar name was the Chinese naturalists' belief that they could see character-

Père David's Deer   *Elaphurus davidianus*

istics of each creature in this animal: a deer's head and legs, a goat's hooves, an ox's body, a horse's tail – and yet they did not believe this animal was any of these.

Now known as Père David's Deer (*Elaphurus davidianus*), the animal has been definitely categorized as a member of the deer family, although a very unusual one, and the only representative of its genus *Elaphurus*. It is a very large deer: 1.2m (4ft) high at the withers, about 1.5m (5ft) long and weighing 200kg (440lb). It is particularly notable for its horse-like tail, and its large dual-branched antlers. It carries its head low like a Caribou and it is the only deer which sheds its antlers twice a year.

At the time of Père David's residence, the animal was virtually unknown, even among Chinese scholars, because for many centuries it was strictly an imperial animal and, quite literally, the possession of the emperors of China. Père David's discovery of the animal was largely accidental. He had long heard of the wonderful imperial nature park of Nan Hai-Tsu, but was unable to gain entry to the preserve. It was strictly forbidden that anyone enter the Emperor's park; punishment for entering it or killing any animal within was death. The park was surrounded by a tall stone wall over 72km (45 miles) long and patrolled by Mongolian guardsmen who would severely punish anyone who even dared to peer over the wall into the park.

These obstacles, however, were not enough to dissuade such a passionate zoologist as Père David. By means of bribery and stealth, Père David safely climbed up on the high wall and was able to view all that lay within the forbidden park. His attention was immediately drawn to the herds of the Ssepu Hsiang which he instantly realized was an animal unknown in the West. Much excited by his discovery, Père David attempted to find out everything he could about the animal.

Its origins were unknown, but it had evidently been

extinct in the wild for many centuries, and the few hundred animals in the emperor's possession in that secret walled garden were all that existed in the world. Without imperial protection, the species would certainly have vanished centuries before it even had the opportunity of being noted and classified by scientists.

After further investigation, Père David learned that the Mongol guards occasionally killed an animal for its meat and antlers. The priest was then able to find a means of bribing the guards into supplying him with two complete skins, which he was able to send off to the zoologist Alphonse Milne-Edward, who wasted no time in naming the animal after the good priest and declaring it a new species previously unknown to science.

In the light of this pronouncement, the French ambassador along with a number of other European ambassadors made formal requests on behalf of their governments for living specimens of these imperial deer for their own national zoos. At first the requests were refused outright, but the power of the Chinese emperors was not what it once was, and eventually about a dozen animals were sent to various European nations. These animals seemed to breed easily in captivity, and with the imperial herd still intact in China, it seemed that the species was very likely to survive for many centuries more.

Sadly, the fortunes of the imperial deer were absolutely linked to the fortunes of the emperors, and by the end of the nineteenth century there was not much hope for either. In 1895, a cataclysmic flood devastated the region around Peking and caused the collapse of the wall which surrounded the imperial reserve. The number of guardsmen by then were too few to do much in the way of protection or even repair of the wall. Most of the deer, attempting to escape the flood, fled and were slaughtered by starving peasants. A small group of thirty or more deer still survived within one walled corner of the park where the remaining guardsmen could give them some protection. This protection only lasted another five years and, in 1900, European troops under the command of the German General Waldersee marched into Peking to put a bloody end to the Boxer Rebellion. The European troops not only slaughtered the Chinese rebels, they also broke into the imperial reserve and killed and ate the last of the imperial herd. Only one solitary deer survived 1900 and it was this lonely animal which remained on display in an enclosure in the Peking Zoo until its death in 1920.

By 1920 there were no animals left in European zoos either. Through astonishingly short-sighted and incompetent handling of the animals in national zoos throughout Europe, all the animals in these collections were now gone. Although they had seemed to breed easily at first in captivity, they proved to need the comfort of the herd to thrive. Zoos tended to keep only one breeding pair and sell off these rare and valuable animals one at a time for short-term profit. A great number of individual animals were isolated in zoos and unable to breed and when the original breeding couples also died, the zoos were suddenly astonished to find there were no animals left – almost.

By great good fortune, Britain's Duke of Bedford was one enlightened collector of rare animals who did not follow this short-sighted policy. A passionate amateur zoologist, the Duke did not have direct access to the animal from China, but began to buy the 'surplus' deer European zoos were so foolishly selling off to anyone who would pay for them. Eventually, the Duke acquired eighteen animals for his estate at Woburn Abbey and this collection of animals proved to be the salvation of the species. He did not cage the animals as nearly all the other zoos did, but allowed them to wander his large estate, much as they had done in the emperor's park in China. Fortunately, the climate and rather swampy grounds of Woburn were comparable to its natural habitat and, able to congregate in substantial herds, the deer began to thrive.

The Duke had always been rather secretive about his prize herd of Père David's Deer, so in 1920 many zoologists thought the animal was extinct. When he revealed that there were over fifty animals in his private collection at Woburn Abbey, they were incredulous. In fact, the Duke had nearly ninety animals before the beginning of World War I, but through an inability to obtain winter fodder, nearly half of them starved to death.

The health of the fifty surviving animals was revived in peacetime, and by 1932 the Woburn herd had grown to nearly two hundred. Wishing to make sure Père David's Deer would never again come so near extinction, the Duke sold considerable numbers of animals so independent herds could be established in a large number of regions.

Today, there are in excess of a thousand Père David's Deer in scores of parks and zoos around the world, although the largest herd still remains at Woburn Abbey. In recent years, a number of these animals have been returned to China in the hope that herds of these unique deer may once again roam freely in that now restored garden of Nan Hai-Tsu.

CHAPTER 6

Banning the Hunt

Whooping and
Other Cranes

'If you've seen fifteen Whooping Cranes, you've seen them all.' In 1941, this statement was literally true. There were only fifteen of these tall, elegant cranes left in the world. Despite all efforts to help them, by 1962, after decades of total protection, these distinctive white cranes with red and black markings had increased in numbers to only twenty-eight. This was an improvement but the fact remained that the entire species was limited to a single flock of birds that twice a year ran the gauntlet of a 4,200km (2,600 mile) migration route from northern Canada to southern Texas. All that was needed was one fierce storm, a serious pollution incident, or even one enthusiastic gang of hunters, to obliterate the species.

One of North America's rarest birds, the Whooping Crane (*Grus americana*) at four feet in height is the tallest bird on the continent. It is also one of the most beautiful and distinctive of birds. This large, sturdy wading bird has snow-white plumage, long black legs, and an equally long, elegant neck. It has a strong spear-like beak for hunting fish, reptiles and crayfish and digging for roots in its swamp-land habitat. Its face and head have very striking crimson markings. The bird takes its name from the 'whooping' sound it makes, especially during its courtship

Whooping Crane   *Grus americana*

dance. This very loud cry can be heard up to 5km (3 miles) away.

Once numbering in the thousands, these great birds were shot by hunters in large numbers each year during their annual migration. Although they were not particularly good food, there was some value in their long white feathers. Hunters of other bird species who just could not resist such large and obvious targets also killed them in large numbers.

It was almost entirely the excesses of these hunters that needlessly brought the Whooping Crane to near extinction. Control, however, was difficult because, like many species, its migration pattern took it through more than one sovereign nation. It was obvious that for the sake of the Whooping Crane and many other endangered birds, co-ordinated international agreements would have to be arranged.

The result was the first international ornithological treaty between two nations: in 1916 the United States and Canada signed the Migratory Bird Convention Act. Later, in 1922, another migratory bird convention was signed between North America and Europe, and in 1936 still another between the United States and Mexico. It was beginning to be realized that conservation – particularly of migratory species – was an international matter.

Such conventions are, however, only the theoretical aspect of conservation efforts; the policing and control of hunters is another matter. In the case of the Whooping Cranes, despite its supposed legal protection, in 1940 and 1941 hunters killed nearly half the breeding population. A massive public education programme was instituted by the governments of both Canada and the United States to let the general public know of the bird's protected status and the critical condition of its population. Known hunting regions on its migration route were particularly well policed. Hunting of Whooping Cranes had now almost ceased entirely, but populations had been driven so low that protection alone was not sufficient to revive their numbers. Radical steps were needed to boost their reproduction rate.

In 1967, the Canadian Wildlife Service started a programme of nest robbing. This began with a strategy similar to the 'double clutching' system used in the captive rearing of other bird species. Many bird species are equipped with a survival system which allows them to lay eggs twice in a single season if the first clutch of eggs is destroyed. Ornithologists took advantage of this by stealing the first batch of eggs and raising them in an incubator, while the wild parents laid a second clutch and raised them as usual. This made it possible to double the number of chicks per nesting couple. The Whooping Crane did not have this ability to lay a second clutch in the same season, and although they nearly always laid two eggs, almost without exception only one of the resultant chicks survived.

With this fact in mind, wildlife wardens made helicopter raids on nesting sites in Canada's Wood Buffalo National Park. The raiders took one egg from each nest and stored them in special heated pouches. They then loaded the eggs on a jet aircraft and flew them to the Patuxent Wildlife Research Center in Laurel, Maryland, where a special breeding facility had been set up.

In the first six years, sixty eggs were collected and over twenty birds survived. Furthermore, for the first time, two of the captive birds between them laid and hatched an egg. In the same year, 1975, an extremely novel foster-parent programme was put into effect. This was a programme of taking some of these 'surplus' Whooping Crane eggs and putting them in the nests of their nearest relatives, the slightly smaller but more numerous Sandhill Cranes.

Much to the surprise of many ornithologists, the experiment has been extremely successful. Despite the obvious difference in size and colour, Sandhill parents have reared and protected the Whoopers as their own. Even more importantly, the fostering programme seems to be resulting in the establishment of other populations with different migration patterns to the main flock. The eventual plan is to establish several populations of Whooping Cranes with different nesting and wintering grounds and different migration patterns, to help protect the species against the possibility of extinction through a single natural or man-made disaster.

It is ironic that, like many critically endangered species today, the only possibility of survival for the Whooping Crane seems to be in the hands of the same species that nearly extinguished it in the first place.

By 1977, only eight years after the egg-collection policy had been instigated, a record number of 126 Whooping Cranes were counted. It was the largest population to be in existence for sixty years or more and it was seemingly healthy with many surviving young birds, each looking forward to a full twenty-five years of life.

That same year, 1977, another group of crane researchers at the newly established International Crane Foundation in Baraboo, Wisconsin, seized the public imagination with their innovative methods, attempting to get artificially inseminated cranes to lay eggs. Working in co-ordination with the Patuxent Center, George Archibald and Ron Sauer established the ICF with their stated aim as being to 'save the cranes of the world'.

Both men were Cornell University graduates. Archibald's degree was, appropriately enough, in crane behaviour. Perhaps inspired by the Cornell falcon experiments, George Archibald used a novel method of approaching the unusual problems which hinder crane reproduction. The difficulty with cranes was not so much in obtaining sperm from males or in inseminating captive females. The real problem was that females must perform their ritual dances with a male in order to become sufficiently excited to produce an egg.

The problem with many captive-reared female birds is that they are not interested in male cranes. They have been 'imprinted' on humans rather than on other cranes. Consequently, they will not involve themselves in a ritual mating dance with a male crane, and are, therefore, unable to lay eggs.

One such bird was a female crane called Tex who was raised as a chick in 1967 in the San Antonio Zoo. She was later taken to Patuxent with the hope that she would breed. The trouble was, Tex showed no interest in other cranes. As one of the researchers explained: 'She thinks she's a person.'

When Archibald visited the centre, he found that she seemed to be especially attracted to him. In 1977, Archibald had Tex transferred to Baraboo and the two became a nationally famous 'odd couple'. Each spring they regularly performed the ritual Whooping Crane mating dances that Tex had refused to do with other Whooping Cranes, but was more than happy to do with Archibald.

These ritual dances were performed for several years, but it was not until 1981 that these intensive pre-natal aerobics paid off. After artificially inseminating her, Archibald lived with Tex for six weeks. For a month Archibald danced with her several times a day. He also foraged for food and gathered twigs to help Tex build her nest. Finally Tex laid an egg, and two and a half weeks later the egg hatched. The little Whooper survived his unorthodox conception and was named Gee Whiz.

For Archibald and the Crane Foundation, Whooping Cranes are just one of the many crane species in serious trouble. The Foundation, by paying close attention to crane behaviour patterns, has achieved considerable success in its captive breeding programme. By 1980, ICF was already captive rearing twenty-five rare cranes a year. Since they began their programme ICF has captive-bred specimens for all fifteen of the world's crane species, including the rare Japanese Red-crowned Crane and the even rarer Siberian Crane. Indeed, the ICF was the first institute to successfully hatch and fledge a captive Siberian Crane. This was a chick named Dushenka.

Despite his remarkable success in the breeding of captive cranes, Archibald recognizes such programmes for what they are: first-aid efforts in the midst of a disaster. He also realizes that the acquisition and maintenance of a suitable wild natural habitat in which hunting is prohibited is the only long-term guarantee that a species will be saved for future generations.

It is for this reason that Archibald considers ICF's greatest success to date the saving of a unique wild habitat for cranes. ICF played a crucial role in getting the Han River estuary – in the uninhabited demilitarized zone which separates North and South Korea – declared a 40 sq. km (15 sq. mile) marsh park for rare cranes and other endangered bird species. It is ironic that endangered birds find safety from hunters' guns in a demilitarized war zone between two hostile nations.

CHAPTER 7

Market-place Embargo

Egret and Sea Otter

On the morning of the 8 July 1905, a wildlife officer for the National Audubon Society took his skiff out into a Florida Everglades bird sanctuary to investigate a schooner anchored near Oyster Key, just off the tip of the Florida mainland. Thirty-five-year-old Guy Bradley was one of the four wardens employed by the newly formed society in the Everglades to enforce the laws banning the slaughter of endangered Egrets (*Leucophoyx thula*).

When Bradley reached the schooner, he discovered two hunters loading dead Egrets aboard. When he attempted to arrest the hunters, the ship's skipper pulled out a gun and shot him. The schooner fled, leaving Bradley dead and adrift in his skiff. His body was discovered by two boys the following day. Bradley's murderer, through some extraordinary legal manoeuvring, was allowed a claim of self-defence and was subsequently set free.

The tragedy of Bradley's murder provided considerable momentum in the drive to have Egret feathers banned in New York's millinery trade. The incident helped to turn the public against the wanton slaughter of these beautiful birds for the sole purpose of supplying feathers for ladies' hats.

At the time of Bradley's death the millinery trade was

responsible for the killing of five million birds annually. Its demands for exotic plumage to decorate hats created a market for every kind of feather, from the tiny Humming-bird to the huge Whooping Crane. A sudden craze for a particular type of exotic feather could, and often did, result in a killing frenzy of such remarkable ferocity that it was actually the cause of species' extinction.

At the turn of the century, the Egret looked as if it would be such a fashion victim. Egret plumage with its long silky filigrees of trailing feathers was the most sought after of all millinery decoration. Indeed, at the turn of the century Egret feathers sold for an incredible thirty-eight dollars an ounce. In the market prices of the day, Egret feathers were quite literally worth their weight in gold.

In one season in Florida alone, records show 130,000 Egrets were slaughtered on their nesting sites. This was a double tragedy, for not only were the 130,000 adults killed, but as the Audubon Society president William Dutcher wrote at the time: 'Women must remember that these birds wear the coveted plumes only during the breeding season, and that the parent birds must be shot in order to obtain the plumes. The young birds in the nest must starve, in consequence of the death of the parents.'

Ironically, the shot that killed Bradley also delivered a death blow to the trade in Egret feathers, for it prompted William Dutcher to point the accusing finger. 'Heretofore, the price has been the life of birds. Now human blood has been added.' Soon after Bradley's death, laws were pushed through in New York, the centre of the millinery trade, prohibiting the use of wild bird feathers in the decoration of hats. Thus the Egret was saved from extinction largely through the bravery and sacrifice of that one wildlife officer, Guy Bradley.

It was the market-place that nearly exterminated the Egret, and it was the closing of that same market-place that was largely responsible for saving that and scores of other species. If concerned citizens had not fought for a market embargo and the feather trade had been allowed to continue, there is no doubt the Egret and many other bird species would not be with us now. If there is one thing that the extinction of the Passenger Pigeon should have taught mankind, it is the ultimate truth that no animal species, however numerous, can withstand the pressure of uncontrolled market hunting. The Passenger Pigeon was the most successful and numerous species of bird on the planet, yet about fifty years of systematic, uncontrolled market hunting was sufficient to exterminate it entirely.

At the turn of the century, the feather trade was quite as large and powerful as the fur trade, but it was fortunately destroyed before it could exterminate all of the species on which it depended. The trade in wild furs has, unfortunately, continued. As with the millinery trade, the fur trade is based on rather frivolous conventions and fads which can be quite deadly to the species currently in fashion. The fashion for beaver hats, for instance, was responsible for almost wiping out that once plentiful species. At one point, extinction looked certain for the beaver, for despite the dramatic collapse in populations, no restrictions of any force were put on the market-places. The beaver was, however, saved – not through any concern about the animal in the industry, but because suddenly fashion changed, and the demand for beaver hats collapsed. The whimsical mad hatters of France and Italy simply decided that silk hats should now be all the rage. What one moment was an absolute necessity to European fashion was merely irrelevant the next.

The trade in wild furs, of course, is still very much with us – with certain restrictions. The recent campaigns against the selling of the pelts of white-coated baby seals have been effective in essentially closing the market-places of Europe and America. They have also largely forced the seal hunters to stop killing the seal pups during their first weeks of life when they lie helplessly at their mothers' sides on the ice floes.

Another of the passing market-place fads in the fur trade at the turn of the century nearly exterminated one of the most charming and likeable animals on the planet. The Sea Otter (*Enhydra lutris*) was believed to be already extinct when an international treaty and ban on selling its pelts was instituted, but it was that treaty that eventually saved the species.

This Sea Otter, at up to 42kg (100lb) is the heaviest member of the otter family. It can measure 1.5m (5ft) in length. In common with other otters it has webbed fore-feet and a strong, muscular tail. Its prized fur is made up from two layers – a thick, short, soft undercoat like velvet, which provides a dense insulating layer, and an upper coat of longer, more wiry hairs which give the coat its water-proof qualities. In colour it can range from a warm chestnut brown to a rich black. It was the richness of these dual-layer coats which caused the Sea Otters to come dangerously close to extinction.

The Sea Otter is an extraordinarily gregarious animal and lives in large family groups. It seems to be constantly at play with members of the family. As mating can occur in any season, pups always seem to be present. When on land, the pups are usually carried by the parents in much the manner a mother cat will carry her young in her mouth. Most of the time, however, the animals are in the water and if the pups tire, the parents swim on their backs allowing the pups to rest on their bellies. The Sea Otter's diet is largely sea urchins, molluscs, shellfish and seaweed. The Sea Otter is one of the few 'tool-using' sea mammals.

Sea Otter   *Enhydra lutris*

When it dives for shellfish, it also brings large flat stones to the surface, then floats on its back and places the stone on its breast. It takes the shell in its paws and strikes the shell hard against the stone and continues this action until the shell breaks and it can eat the contents of the shell. Often otters can be heard tapping away with the shells on the stones while floating around far from the shore.

Sea Otters rarely come to the shore, preferring to live in the water around floating kelp beds; the females even have their young in the water. Unlike any other marine mammal, the Sea Otter's usual floating position is on its back and this, not incorrectly, makes observers think of it as having a casual, relaxed and generally 'laid-back' personality. They certainly are the most charming, playful and intelligent of sea mammals.

When George Steller sailed with Vitus Bering in 1741 on that first Russian expedition through the North Pacific, the Steller's Sea Cow was only one of many wonderful new creatures which he discovered. When he returned home with stories of the things that he had seen, he also carried with him pelts of the Sea Otter. The Russians, as leading fur merchants of the time, were quick to recognize the potential of these animals and soon sent their ships off in search of them. The British and Americans quickly followed suit and although fur seals were the main prey, the Sea Otters were also taken as a luxury item, and in enormous quantities.

In the thirty-year period of 1790 to 1820 Russian ships took 200,000 Sea Otter pelts out of the North Pacific, but this was only the beginning. In 1867, the United States purchased Alaska from the Russians. During the second half of the century the Americans killed 50,000 Sea Otters a year, while Russians and British made their own substantial slaughters in the Aleutians and British Columbia.

Prices rose to over $1,000 dollars a skin, a phenomenal price when labourers were being paid as little as a dollar a week.

During the one hundred and fifty years of unrestricted slaughter, about one million Sea Otters were killed for their skins. By 1900, the animals were virtually extinct and the market had collapsed. A treaty was finally signed by America, Russia, Britain and Japan, but this appeared at first to be a largely empty gesture. The opposition of the fur marketeers to the treaty stopped only because they had not received a single pelt for several years and, cynically, they had nothing to lose by the treaty. Many of the fur traders, as well as the conservationists, believed the animal was extinct.

However, they were not quite right as a number of years later there were sightings on a remote Russian island. And in 1936, nearly thirty years after Sea Otters were last seen in American waters, they were sighted off Amchitka Island, and that population was immediately placed under protection and allowed to grow. It grew with surprising rapidity and over the next three or four decades colonized other areas of Alaska and British Columbia. Another remarkable discovery was made in California in 1938 when a colony of some ninety animals was sighted off Monterey. Sea Otters were believed to have been extinct south of British Columbia for at least seventy years. Although the southern colony did not expand as rapidly as the northern population, it has maintained a certain stability despite adverse conditions and hostility from local fishermen.

In November 1971, despite widespread opposition, the American military invaded the Amchitka Island nature reserve and used it as the test site for the ignition of a huge underground nuclear bomb. In Canada, in particular, there was considerable outrage because not only was this an area set aside to protect Alaska's largest single Sea Otter colony, it was a wildlife refuge for a number of other endangered species. It was also on a notoriously active earthquake fault line. The movement of this fault had, a few years earlier, caused a tidal wave which had seriously damaged Canadian coastal towns.

One of the most memorable events in this conflict was the direct-action tactics of the then unknown group of Canadian activists who called themselves Greenpeace. Amchitka was their very first campaign and they sailed a protest boat into the test zone.

The nuclear explosion may have given birth to Greenpeace, but it proved to be the end for the Amchitka Sea Otters. Although the military lied about the explosion's effects at the time, the blast killed over a thousand animals: the entire Amchitka population. Fortunately, the population had colonized itself elsewhere by then, and soon the overall population began to show signs of recovery again.

In 1972, the US Congress passed further legislation to protect Sea Otters by introducing the Marine Mammal Protection Act, which established a moratorium on the killing of any marine mammals without a special permit. Other federal laws now exist which prohibit even the possession of a Sea Otter pelt without a permit.

With the market for animal fur now outlawed, the Sea Otters' main enemy these days is pollution – as the 1989 Alaskan oil spill disaster has demonstrated. Oil can be a major killer for these animals as it destroys the water-proofing and insulating quality of their fur, and the Sea Otter either drowns or dies of cold. However, the pollution factor put aside, the Sea Otters' salvation has been the banning of the market on its fur. Today the Californian population is just under 2,000 and the North Pacific population is 40,000 – and still growing.

CHAPTER 8

Habitat Preservation

American Bison and Wisent

The great buffalo herds of North America were one of the natural wonders of the world. The American Buffalo (*Bison bison*) – or more properly, the Bison – is that continent's largest land animal. It is 1.8m (6ft) tall at the shoulder, nearly 3.6m (12ft) in length and weighs more than one ton. Estimates of its numbers at the time of European contact and up until 1800 were in excess of sixty million animals, making it the largest congregation of any single species of land animals on the planet.

One traveller named Thomas Farham wrote in 1839 that on the Santa Fe Trail it took him three days to ride peacefully through only a part of a single Bison herd. He estimated the herd to be standing on a grazing area of 3,500 sq. km (1,350 sq. miles) – roughly the area of the state of Rhode Island. The herd was considerably in excess of a million animals. As late as 1871, the famous gunfighter (and one-time buffalo hunter) Wyatt Earp described a similar scene, again involving more than a million animals: 'I could see twenty or thirty miles in each direction. For all that distance the range seemed literally packed with grazing Buffaloes. The prairie appeared to be covered by a solid mass of their woolly heads and humps, flowing along like a great muddy river. Clear to the horizon the herd was endless.'

At the time of Wyatt Earp's description, Bison outnumbered the human inhabitants of the continent, but within nine short years, the vast herds had entirely vanished. Contrary to popular belief, the disappearance of the Bison did not come about unforeseen. It was, in fact, a planned extermination. The American military, in particular, encouraged and rewarded those who slaughtered Bison simply for sport or for their tongues and hides. It had been the unofficial military and government policy actively to seek the Bison's extinction. One Congressman claimed the Bison must go because 'they are as uncivilized as the Indians'.

The connection with the Indian was not an arbitrary one, but the real reason behind the slaughter. As General Sheridan wrote at the time: 'The Buffalo Hunters have done more in the last two years to settle the vexed Indian

Bison   *Bison bison*

Question than the entire regular army in the last thirty years. They are destroying the Indians' commissary. Send them powder and lead, if you will, and let them kill, skin and sell until they have exterminated the buffalo.' Sheridan later told Congress it should mint a bronze medal for the skin hunters, with a dead Bison on one side and an Indian on the other.

The killing was carried out at an astonishing pace. During the thirty years between 1850 and 1880, more than seventy-five million buffalo hides were sold to American dealers. Practically none of these animals was used, as the Indians used them, for food.

The legendary hunter Buffalo Bill Cody claimed the greatest number of Bison killed by any one man in a year. He killed 4,862 Bison in one year. Had these animals been as efficiently marketed as domestic cattle, this individual's efforts could have fed the entire population of San Francisco of that time for nearly two weeks.

By 1880 the great hunt was over, and there was virtually nothing left. The Black Bison (*Bison bison pennsylvanicus*) of Eastern United States was extinct by 1825, and the Oregon Bison (*Bison bison oreganus*) of the far West was exterminated by 1850. That only left the Great Plains (*Bison bison bison*) and the Northern Wood (*Bison bison athabasca*) Bisons, and both these subspecies were so severely reduced that there seemed virtually no chance of their survival.

In 1889, the American government policy of intentional extermination was reversed, and a rescue plan was launched. America's last free-roaming wild Bison were captured that year and put on protective reserves, most of them in Yellowstone National Park. However, these herds were in very poor health, and by 1900 their population had dwindled to just thirty-nine animals.

It was through the considerable efforts of William T.

Hornaday, the director of the New York Zoological Park and the foremost conservationist of the day, that the American Bison did not become extinct. Hornaday founded the American Bison Society and raised large amounts of money to promote breeding programmes and allow these stranded herds, deprived of the freedom to migrate to warmer southern grasslands during the winter, to be fed and sheltered.

The secret to the Bison's survival, Hornaday knew, was land. If suitable habitats were not secured for these last Bison, the species was doomed. The society reached a turning point in 1905 when President Theodore Roosevelt threw his support behind it, and new parkland was assigned. Luckily Bison are strong breeders, and once substantial parkland was granted in many states (even in Alaska), the animals made a phenomenal recovery.

In Canada, a number of parks were established for Bison, the two largest being Wainright National Buffalo Park and Wood Buffalo National Park in Alberta and the Northwest Territories. (Wood Buffalo Park is certainly the largest Bison park in the world, covering an area roughly the size of Belgium.) There are now nearly 40,000 Bison living in parklands throughout the continent – about 80 per cent of these in the big Canadian reserves. And although the legendary herds of the last century will never again be seen, the survival and revival of these substantial populations must be considered one of the great victories of the conservation movement.

Like the native American tribal peoples who were mis-named Indians because Christopher Columbus believed he had sailed all the way round the world to the East Indies, the American Bison was called a buffalo because of his resemblance to the African and Asian Water-buffalo. This seems a curious mistake, because the American

Bison far more closely resembles its cousin, the European Wisent.

In fact, the European Wisent is more properly a European Bison (*Bison bonasus*), and the story of its narrow escape from extinction is even more harrowing than that of the American Bison.

The Wisent once lived throughout forested areas of Europe and could be found in the forests of Germany, Poland, Hungary and Caucasian Russia. The Wisent has a fawn-coloured coat, less 'woolly' or shaggy-maned than the American Bison and its forequarters are less massive. Both animals weigh over a ton, but the Wisent is taller, its body longer, less barrel-like, and its hindquarters are larger and stronger.

By the 1800s Wisent populations surviving in the wild had dwindled to small herds in only two regions. One subspecies was to be found in the Caucasus region of Russia while the other race survived in the Bialowieska Forest of Poland. Both the Caucasian Wisent (*Bison bonasus caucasicus*) and the Polish Wisent (*Bison bonasus bonasus*) populations survived because they lived in substantial park reserves which were under the protection of the Czar of Russia.

The two herds numbered about a thousand animals each but when the land was devastated by the Great War and the Russian Revolution and the Czar's protection was no longer a deterrent, local poachers moved in. Worse still, Russian and Polish troops used military weapons and vehicles to slaughter the last few surviving wild Wisent.

In 1923, the Polish zoologist Jan Sztolcman was alerted to the near extinction of the Wisent. In imitation of the American model, he founded the European Bison Society at the Berlin Zoo. Without his group's actions, there is no doubt the European Bison would have entirely vanished.

By 1923, both subspecies of the Wisent had become

extinct in the wild, yet Sztolcman continued to work towards the preservation of the species through captive breeding. In spite of his efforts, however, in 1925 an ageing bull called Kaukasus, the last of the Caucasian race, died in the Hamburg Zoo without mating.

Sztolcman's Bison Society was more fortunate with the northern race of Wisent, managing to acquire a total of six captive animals from three different collections, to form the nucleus of a breeding group. It also located a few animals in ten other European collections, with the largest herd being the twenty animals which lived on the estate of the Duke of Bedford at Woburn Abbey. In total, the world population of the northern Wisent was less than fifty, a large proportion of which were beyond breeding age.

The Bison Society was determined to keep the Wisent alive despite enormous obstacles. Like the American Bison Society, it arranged for an international breeding programme, although the problems were far more complex. By 1938, there were one hundred animals in existence, when war again intervened, driving the population down to less than seventy.

Since the end of the Second World War, new parklands have been established to give room for them to breed and their numbers have increased steadily. Today, there are nearly three thousand European Bison roaming woodland parks and reserves in Europe. Like their American cousins, the Wisent have proved very strong breeders and so long as their natural habitat is preserved, they can substantially revive their populations. Interestingly enough, the largest Wisent herd in the world roams in the woodlands of the Bialowieska Forest, that very same reserve in Poland that was once protected by Czarist soldiers before the First World War.

CHAPTER 9

Returned to the Wild

Arabian Oryx and
Peregrine Falcon

'Operation Oryx' was one of the most dramatic of the World Wildlife Fund's early search-and-rescue operations. The programme was a remarkable success because it not only succeeded in sustaining the Arabian Oryx (*Oryx leucoryx*) through captive breeding when it had become extinct in the wild, but after overcoming many obstacles it was actually able to build up a new wild population by reintroducing captive animals back into their traditional habitat.

The Arabian Oryx, often considered the most beautiful of the world's antelopes, is a large, cream-coloured desert antelope with black markings and magnificent, 90cm (35in), spiralling horns. It measures about 1m (3ft) at the withers and weighs about 100kg (220lb). It is fast and strong. It is capable of surviving for weeks without drinking water and it can cover incredible distances in a short time. It is also capable of defending itself from most natural predators by lowering its head and spearing its enemies with those formidable horns.

The Arabian Oryx once roamed throughout the desert lands of the Middle East. However, relentless hunting resulted in its being eliminated by the twentieth century from all its habitats except the Rub al-Khali, the 'empty quarter' of the great southern desert of Arabia, Aden and Oman.

By the 1950s, even these remote surviving Oryx herds came under extreme pressure, as wealthy Arab hunters organized large motorized hunting parties. These hunters found it amusing to use automatic machine guns to shoot the fleeing Oryx from speeding jeeps or even aeroplanes and helicopters.

In 1961, when it was estimated that there were less than one hundred Arabian Oryx left in the world, a single party of wealthy hunters from Qatar on the Persian Gulf entered Eastern Aden and, over several weeks, tracked down and killed no less than forty-eight Oryx.

It was following this massacre that conservationists felt a major effort must be made to save the species. In 1962, the International Union for the Conservation of Nature, the Fauna Preservation Society and the World Wildlife Fund launched 'Operation Oryx'. An expedition headed by Major Ian Grimwood was sent into the desert to track down and capture a herd of Oryx in order to establish a captive breeding programme.

The expedition revealed that the plight of the Arabian Oryx was far more serious than even the worst estimates had suggested. In six thousand miles of desert, the searchers could only locate four Oryx. With considerable difficulty, these four animals were captured alive – but only three survived. One died shortly after capture from a bullet which had remained in its body from a previous encounter with hunters.

At enormous expense, the three wild Oryx were flown to a safe refuge of a similar desert habitat in a special breeding unit of the Phoenix Zoo in Arizona. There they were joined by one captive animal from the London Zoo, one from the Sultan of Kuwait's zoo, and four from King Saud's private collection. These nine animals were called

Arabian Oryx   *Oryx leucoryx*

the World Herd, and were the nucleus of the captive breeding operation. In less than fifteen years, the captive population grew to over one hundred healthy animals, and breeders were sure that the critical period was over.

Meanwhile, in the Arabian desert, the 'empty quarter' became even emptier still. Operation Oryx was indeed an eleventh hour rescue plan, for the animal became extinct in the wild soon after. The last three Arabian Oryx ever seen in the wild were shot in 1972. The Arabian Oryx was not the only victim of these senseless hunts as most other forms of large game had also been eliminated. By the mid-sixties both the Arabian Ostrich and the Syrian Onager (or wild ass) had, similarly, been hunted down to extinction.

Luckily, by the 1980s the Arabian Oryx had bred so successfully in captivity that the decision was made to reintroduce captive animals into certain protected wild regions. Release sites were chosen in Israel, Jordan and the wilderness of Jiddat-al-Harasis in Oman. The governments of each nation have set aside land and have taken reasonable security measures. In Oman, for instance, the local Harasis tribesmen are effectively employed as rangers to guard the herd from poachers.

Reports from these regions conclude happily that the captive Arabian Oryx have readily adapted back into the wild, exhibiting typical feral Oryx behaviour patterns and the ability to hold their own against natural enemies and the elements. The possibility of large Arabian Oryx herds once again roaming the deserts of the Near East is no longer simply a conservationists' dream, but a practical and likely eventuality.

In the bird world, there is a similar success story to that of the Arabian Oryx. This is the story of a rescue programme organized at Cornell University to rescue the endangered

Peregrine Falcon (*Falco peregrinus*), the swiftest and most remarkable member of the falcon family.

In 1970, a professor of ornithology named Tom Cade established the Peregrine Fund as a long-term programme of research at Cornell University in order to learn how to propagate rare falcons in captivity. The programme was organized in response to the increasing rarity of Peregrine and other falcons in the wild.

The Peregrine is a bird celebrated for its hundred-mile-an-hour hunting dives, its speed and its skill. Since the time of the ancient Egyptians, the Peregrine has been the falconer's favourite bird but by 1970 ornithologists were giving up on the Peregrine Falcon's chances of survival. It was clearly a vanishing species and they felt there was no chance of recovery. By that time the Peregrine was extinct in Eastern United States and in the West there were less than a hundred birds, and most of these were incapable of producing young.

The reason for the disappearance of the Peregrine was the wide use of pesticides. It took nearly twenty years for scientists to understand what was going on, but by the late sixties it was shown that DDE, a breakdown component of DDT, interferes with calcium production. In predatory birds, like falcons, the presence of DDE in even the most minute quantities resulted in the production of thin-shelled eggs that could not withstand the weight of the nesting female bird. Consequently, no new chicks could be born to contaminated birds.

It took until 1972 to have DDT banned in America, but by then it seemed that it was too late for the Peregrine. Similar declines were being observed in Peregrine populations throughout its range in Scandinavia, Russia and Western Europe.

In North America, the American Peregrine had two cousins that made their homes outside areas that had heavy pesticide usage. These were the subspecies called the Arctic Peregrine and Peale's Peregrine. Unfortunately, the Arctic subspecies was also slowly building up critical levels of contamination on its annual southward migrations to South America. The only healthy subspecies seemed to be the non-migratory Peale's Peregrine on the relatively remote Queen Charlotte Islands in British Columbia.

At this time Tom Cade and a few other falcon enthusiasts believed that they had nothing left to lose by attempting some sort of breeding programme with a few healthy captive Peregrines. Most experts gave them little chance of success. After attempting it for centuries, only three or four falconers had ever bred the Peregrines in captivity, and these were widely considered one-off flukes which could not be seriously considered as a basis for a large-scale breeding programme.

However, after three years of trying, in 1973, Tom Cade's team succeeded in breeding twenty captive Peregrines in a single year. Since then, the programme has been amazingly successful. Using a combination of traditional and unconventional approaches to the problems of falcon reproduction, they have bred hundreds of birds in their new expanded facilities.

Furthermore, since the early successes with the Peregrines, Cornell University and other institutes using its methods have successfully bred a large number of birds of prey in captive programmes. Besides Peregrines, there have been successful captive breeding programmes for over fifteen falcon species, including Gyrfalcons, Sakers and Lanners. Other birds of prey that have been taken into captive breeding programmes are the Red-tailed Hawk, Harris' Hawk, Ferruginous Hawk, Osprey, Bateleur, Burrowing Owl, Common Buzzard, Lesser Spotted Eagle, Philippine Monkey-eating Eagle, Bald Eagle and

Golden Eagle. These programmes have given new hope for survival to many of the world's most spectacular birds of prey.

We must remember, though, that captive breeding is only the first stage of these programmes. Like that of the Arabian Oryx, the long-term aim is reintroduction into the wild. The Cornell programme with Peregrines proved sufficiently successful to allow captive birds to be released in selected areas. These birds are now re-establishing themselves in traditional Peregrine territories. Remarkably, they are regaining a foothold in the Eastern United States where they were altogether extinct. It is the first time in ornithological history that a regional population has been revived by captive stock.

It is an ongoing struggle, but for the first time since the 1950s Peregrine Falcons can be seen in eastern America. Not only are they surviving their reintroduction to the wild, but they are now rearing healthy young birds. Even in the great cities of eastern America, they have found they are well-suited to high-rise living and make their eyries on the man-made cliffs of skyscrapers and office-block towers.

Afterword

Today, there are thousands of animal and plant species in danger of extinction. Reading through the first part of this book, you will begin to understand the reasons for this destruction. Reading the second part, you will begin to understand how survival is possible, and that individual and group action against such destruction can succeed.

It is now a critical and dangerous time for environmentalists in their battle to save the species of the planet. Many have literally sacrificed their lives to the cause. As you have read in this book, in 1905 Guy Bradley was murdered in his attempt to save the Egrets of Florida, and in 1985 Dian Fossey was murdered in Rwanda while working to preserve the last Mountain Gorillas.

An equally famous environmental martyr was Joy Adamson, the author of *Born Free*, murdered in 1980 on the Shaba Lion reserve in Kenya. Tragically in 1989 her husband, the distinguished conservationist, George Adamson, was also brutally murdered in Kenya by a well-armed gang of ivory hunters.

But these are only a famous few. In Africa alone several hundred have died, for instance, in pitched gun battles with armies of elephant and rhino poachers. In Brazil between 1986 and 1988, no fewer than 700 forest-dwelling peasant farmers and rubber tappers (and at least as many tribal peoples) were murdered by hired assassins because they attempted to organize a resistance movement against the destruction of the rainforest.

Dangerous as certain aspects of the environmental movement may be, there can be no doubt about the importance of the struggle, and there can be few conflicts on this planet where it is easier to see which side the angels would choose.

The environmental movement is gaining momentum world-wide. I have no doubt at all that a few of you reading this book will, in the years to come, become directly involved in the movement. Indeed, it is possible that some of you may play a crucial role in the saving of some unique species from the oblivion of extinction.

But the few who become directly involved can only be successful if the rest of us give our support and sympathy. We can all join an environmental group – whether it be local, national or international – and keep informed on environmental issues. We can all do a little volunteer work for one of these groups. We can all write letters to governments and industries. If we see a special need, we can even start our own group.

Most important of all, we can refuse to buy products that lead to the destruction of species in the wild. If we simply think about them for a second, most of the choices are easy, and will not lead to any real personal hardship.

Millions of animal deaths could be avoided each year if we all refused to buy ivory, wild-animal furs, and wild-caught exotic pets. Ninety per cent of all elephant, walrus and whale ivory is illegally obtained and is rapidly helping speed all these species towards extinction. The trade in wild furs and skins has already extinguished dozens of wild animal species and critically endangered virtually every species it has exploited. Most wild pets are cruelly and illegally caught, and for every captive chimpanzee, parrot or tropical fish that reaches the pet shop, nine others have died on the way. Of the survivors, nine out of ten of those die within a year.

The simple fact is that by buying these products we are paying the wages of those who slaughter the animals. In such cases as elephant ivory, we are paying murderers of humans as well.

So, even if we feel we can do nothing directly to save a species from extinction, the very least we can do is refuse to finance those who are exterminating it.

We are now only beginning to understand how our own survival is directly at risk. By ignoring the consequences of environmental destruction we have brought upon ourselves a situation which is as perilous as that of the legendary Noah when all the world was drowned in the great flood.

The idea of a universal flood today is not just a metaphor for disaster. If we continue destroying the great oxygen-producing forests of the planet and at the same time keep increasing our pollution of the atmosphere, the result will be what scientists call the 'Greenhouse Effect'. Increased carbon dioxide in the atmosphere will result in a heating up of the earth's temperatures.

The most dramatic result would be the thawing of the polar ice-caps. The release of these huge reservoirs of frozen water would result in the planet's sea-levels rising by 3 to 6m (10 to 20ft).

This would indeed be a flood of biblical proportions. As most of the world's great cities are sea or river ports the homes of over half the human race would be flooded. Furthermore, most of the world's current food-producing regions would either be put under water or turned into deserts by these rapid climatic shifts.

Hopefully, we can learn the lessons of history. By working to save the other species of the planet, we may yet save ourselves. There is little doubt the environment is the most important long-term issue that we are faced with today. The decisions we make as individual citizens, as representatives of governments, as employees and managers of industries during the next few decades, will determine the fate of most of the planet's species – including our own.

Index

Note: Animal species are entered under the common name followed by the Latin name in brackets, where both names are given in the book, e.g. Dodo (*Raphus cucullatus*).

Index

Index

Index

Index

Index

Index

Index

Non-fiction from Dick King-Smith

COUNTRY WATCH

Animal watching can be fascinating and fun – if you know what to look out for and how best to observe it. There are so many different kinds of animals to see in the British countryside and it's not only the unusual ones that are interesting. *Country Watch* is full of surprising facts (did you know that the tiny mole can burrow its way through thirty pounds of earth in an hour?) and Dick King-Smith has lots of marvellous stories to tell about his own encounters with animals over the years.

TOWN WATCH

It's surprising how many wild animals there are to be seen in towns today. *Town Watch* is crammed with information about the many mammals, birds, insects and reptiles that live within the bounds of our towns and cities. Did you know that the cheeky house-sparrow is really one of the tough guys of the bird world, roaming the city in gangster-style mobs? From rubbish-tip pests like rats and cockroaches to protected species such as owls and bats, this book has a wealth of information and stories about urban wildlife.

WATER WATCH

If you look at a map of the world, you'll see that most of its surface is sea. We are surrounded by water – all around us there are lakes, ponds, rivers and streams – not to mention man-made waterways like canals. On holiday at the seaside you can enjoy identifying all the different kinds of gull, or if you're near a rocky coastline you might even see a seal! And there are all sorts of water birds – some with very unusual habits – living near lakes and marshes. You'd have to be lucky to spot an otter but if you're patient and observant, there are some fascinating animals to be spotted in and around a garden or village pond.

THE ALIENS ARE COMING
Phil Gates

The greenhouse effect is warming up the earth so that snowmen could become an endangered species. It also means you may have to eat more ice-cream to keep cool in summer. But worse, it may cause the spread of alien plants which will cause havoc in the countryside and could cause some native plants, which like a cool moist climate, to become extinct.

Find out for yourself, through the experiments and information in this original and entertaining book, just what is happening now and what is likely to happen in the future.

Become a scientist and help warn the world about the dangers ahead!

LAND AHOY! THE STORY OF CHRISTOPHER COLUMBUS
Scoular Anderson

The colour of the sea was probably the last thing that Christopher Columbus was thinking about when he set off, five hundred years ago, on one of the greatest voyages of discovery ever made. His journey was just as adventurous and just as important as the first space flight to the moon was this century. But Columbus set sail into the vast ocean not really knowing where he was going or, once he had got there, what he'd found!

Now you can be an explorer by reading this book and finding out just what an extraordinary man Columbus was – how he managed to travel the world and put America on the map for the first time.

THE ANIMAL QUIZ BOOK
Sally Kilroy

Why do crocodiles swallow stones? Which bird migrates the furthest? Can kangaroos swim? With over a million species, the animal kingdom provides a limitless source of fascinating questions. In this book Sally Kilroy has assembled a feast for enquiring minds – from domestic animals to dinosaurs, fish to footprints, reptiles to record breakers. Discover where creatures live, how they adapt to their conditions, the way they treat each other, the dangers they face – you'll be surprised how much you didn't know.

EUROPE: UP AND AWAY
Sue Finnie

A lively book packed with information about Western Europe which includes sections on stamps, car numbers and languages as well as topics related to an individual country (from Flamenco dancing to frogs' legs).

WATCH OUT: Keeping safe outdoors
Rosie Leyden and Suzanne Ahwai

A book to give children an awareness of the dangers lurking outside on the roads, on their bikes, near water, on building sites, etc. It is full of fun, puzzles and quizzes as well as being packed with information on how to stay safe.

ENVIRONMENTALLY YOURS
Early Times

What is the greenhouse effect? Why is the Earth getting warmer? Who is responsible for the destruction of the countryside? Where can you get advice on recycling? When will the Earth's resources run out? The answers to all these questions and many more are given in this forthright and informative book. Topics such as transport, industry, agriculture, population and energy are covered as well as lists of 'green' organizations and useful addresses.

ANIMAL KIND
Early Times

Animal Kind looks at what humans are doing to animals. It also looks at what humans *could* be doing for animals to make their lives happier and to lessen their suffering. This is a hard-hitting book that covers topics such as vivisection, vegetarianism, farming, wildlife, pets and blood sports. It will help you look again at your relationship to the animal world.

FAME! WHO'S WHO IN HISTORY AT MADAME TUSSAUD'S

Wendy Cooling

Find out about kings, queens, politicians, authors, dictators, idols, plotters and peacemakers. You'll also be able to discover which other famous events happened in the world during the centuries in which they lived.

Some people are only famous for a short time. EVERYONE in this book has earned themselves a lasting place in history and in the most famous hall of fame – Madame Tussaud's.

PETS FOR KEEPS

Dick King-Smith

Keeping a pet can be fascinating and great fun. You don't have to be an expert either. But it is important to choose the right pet: one that will fit in with your family and surroundings, one that you can afford to keep, one that you will enjoy looking after, and – most important – one that will be happy with you. This book is packed with useful information about budgies, hamsters, cats, guinea-pigs, mice, rabbits, gerbils, canaries, bantams, rats, goldfish and dogs.

PUFFIN BOOK OF ROYAL LONDON
Scoular Anderson

Nowadays the word palace can mean any grand building, but this is a book about a very special group of palaces – the Royal Palaces of London – where the kings and queens of Britain lived and where the present Queen lives today.

Find out which were the favourite palaces and which one had a nasty pong; how the royals got about before cars, trains and buses; why they were sometimes sentenced to death and executed at the Tower; what they did for entertainment and what they ate at the royal banquets! Banquets, beefeaters and beheadings abound in this hilarious guide to Royal London.

WELL, WELL, WELL
Dr Peter Rowan

Find out what your body can (and can't) do; how its many parts work together to keep you healthy; what happens when things go wrong and who and what can make you better. Dr Pete gives some top tips on how to keep yourself fit, as well as some breathtaking facts which will amaze and amuse you.